NIGHTMARE

G. LOUISE BEARD

Copyright ©2023 G. Louise Beard

All rights reserved.

ISBN: 978-1-957917-36-8 (paperback)
ISBN: 978-1-957917-37-5 (e-book)

Library of Congress Control Number: 2023911355

All rights reserved. No part of this book may be reproduced, stored in a retrieval system, or transmitted in any form or by any means without prior written permission from the author, except for the use of brief quotations in a book review.

Edited by Vince Font
Cover design by Judith S. Design & Creativity
www.judithsdesign.com
Published by Glass Spider Publishing
www.glassspiderpublishing.com

This book is dedicated to the memory of our parents, Harold and Daisy.

Harold, the son of sharecroppers, was born the eleventh of twelve children. Harold, even though you had only a fourth-grade education, you ensured that each of the five of us (your son and daughters) earned an education beyond high school, with two of us earning post-graduate degrees.

Daisy (Mommy), you started your career as a dessert girl at the hospital where you worked, but after thirty-five years retired as one of the on-site nutritionists.

Thank you both for your guidance and encouragement of working toward taking the steps that allowed us to have the confidence to reach for our goals. Thank you both for guiding us into a Christ-centered faith-based relationship with God.

—G. Louise Beard

CHAPTER 1

Finell Everson stood at the end of a long, dark tunnel dressed in a wedding gown and veil. Music played from somewhere far ahead, where a light at the end of the tunnel beckoned her. Standing in that light was her soon-to-be husband, David Colwins.

Desperately, Finell gathered the hem of her dress in her arms so she could run to him, but she froze. She didn't want the mud and dirt to soil her dress and shoes. She called to David, but he couldn't hear her.

Suddenly, the tunnel disappeared. There was light everywhere, and now she stood in the doorway at the end of the center aisle of the church. David was at the altar, but he was holding another woman's hands.

Finell's eyes fell upon her friends and the congregation. They were all pointing and laughing at her dress, which was covered in mud.

In an instant, her eyes flew open. She was in her bed. Heart racing wildly, Finell pulled her blankets up under her chin as her bottom lip caught between her teeth. She snatched a tissue from the box on her nightstand and wiped the tears from her face.

At least this time, I didn't scream, 'No! He's mine! You can't have him!

Give him back!" she thought.

Finell took a deep breath and wished she could stay in bed for the rest of her life. But only if she could stop herself from having that dream.

At least it's getting better, she reminded herself. *It only happens once or twice a week now instead of every night.*

It was Monday. Another week of getting up, going to work, coming home, crying herself sick, then going to bed and starting the same mundane existence all over again the next day. It had been close to two years since David had broken their engagement and married someone else. But to Finell, it still felt like yesterday.

It happened just after worship service on a Sunday afternoon. As usual, David met her in the parking lot since he didn't attend her church with her. Finell was getting into her car when David approached her. This time, he wasn't alone. This time, there was a woman with him.

As she usually did, Finell smiled at David and leaned in to kiss him, but he took a step backward. That was when she saw David and the woman were holding hands.

"Uh...hello, Finell," David said, stumbling over his words. "This is Abigail... She's... We... Look, this is the end of the relationship between you and me. Our engagement is off. I found someone that makes me very happy, and we're getting married. As you can see, she's nothing like you. She's petite, thin, and beautiful. And she isn't afraid to show me that she loves me. She's been willing to give herself to me since the night we met. So...take care, okay?" As David and his new love walked away, he called back over his shoulder. "I hope you understand. Goodbye. Have a good life."

Feeling angry and embarrassed, Finell wanted the ground to open up and swallow her. She stood looking after the two retreating figures and thought, *Why did he do that to me in public?*

It wasn't the fact she had just been abruptly and rudely dumped, but rather the fact it had been done in such a public way.

He's such a coward! she screamed in her head.

The spectators to this scene, the others who were also getting into their cars, looked at Finell with shocked expressions. All she could do was get into her car and leave the parking lot as soon as she could. It still didn't stop some from pointing at her and telling others what had just transpired.

As Finell pulled into the line of cars waiting to exit the church's parking lot, David returned and tapped on her window. Finell lowered it a crack, and David extended his hand. "Why don't you go ahead and give me that ring? I need to use it as a down payment for Abigail's rings."

Finell glared at David and said, "Why don't you go ahead and get away from me? Go enjoy your new life, David, and leave me alone." She rolled the window back up and pressed the lock button on the door just as David grabbed the handle and pulled.

When his attempt to get to her didn't work, David slapped his hand on the window. "Hand it over, Finell! It's not yours anymore. You have no right to keep it."

With the parking lot traffic at a standstill, Finell had no way to escape David's barrage, and he was beginning to draw the attention of the people who had not yet gotten into their cars. Feeling she had no other recourse, Finell reached for the container of mace in the cupholder on her car door, flipped back the safety cap, and cracked the window.

"David, get away from my car and stop banging on my window, please."

"I'm not going anywhere until you give me what I want," he barked. "Now hand it over, you fat bitch!" He had an expectant look on his face, as if he thought raising his voice and cursing would get him what he wanted.

Finell lowered the car window a little more, leaned back, covered her face with one hand, and with the other sprayed the mace into David's face. Then she dropped the canister and rolled the window back up, leaving David holding his hands over his face and screaming like a girl.

Three men from the church security staff ran up to David and grabbed his arms. One of them motioned for Finell to lower her window. When she did, he told her to park her car and follow them back inside.

The head of security called the police. When they arrived, officers took statements from bystanders and asked Finell if she wanted to press charges. She said she did, and David was arrested.

* * *

Two and a half hours later, Finell was finally able to drive her car off of the church parking lot. After all of that unpleasant activity, sitting in her car driving home gave her a sense of relief.

As the release began to settle into her mind, she let her guard down. Before long, the tears came so hard and fast that she had to pull over. She let them fall until she had no more tears left.

When she got home, she parked in her driveway, too worn and emotionally drained to bother with the hassle of pulling into the garage. She went into her house, locked the door, closed the drapes, and sat on her living room sofa, ignoring the constantly ringing phone and the insistent knocking on her front and back doors.

The next day, Finell went about the business of canceling all of the arrangements for what was supposed to have been her wedding day. Most of the people were willing to refund the deposits since there were still four months before June. The only thing for which she couldn't get a full refund was the honeymoon arrangements, so she reset it as an open reservation for her vacation.

Within three days of the cancellations, David showed up at her door. He demanded to know why she'd voided all the wedding and honeymoon arrangements and insisted that she reset them.

"You had no right to cancel them, Finell, you're wrong and you know it!" David ranted, standing on her front porch. Sighing deeply and sliding his hands into his pockets, he flashed what he thought was one of his most charming smiles. "Don't you want to see me happy, baby? Don't be bitter and vindictive because I found happiness with someone who isn't frigid and afraid of sex."

He was trying to make her feel small for not putting his needs and wants ahead of her own. He'd been so good at that in the past, but Finell was through letting David manipulate her.

"Why don't you have your beautiful, petite, loving fiancée make her own arrangements?"

"Abigail and I are getting married in four weeks," David said, "and we don't have time to make any new plans. We were planning to use all the arrangements you and I made since they were already in place. Besides, we can't afford to make any full wedding and honeymoon arrangements right now."

Hearing David claim he'd had a hand in setting any of their wedding and honeymoon plans made Finell frown, with her brow furrowed, she realized that she was beyond angry. She was furious!

Always taking credit for what others have done, she thought. *I can see now that I'm better off without someone like him in my life. He's just a loser.*

"David," she warned, "get away from my house before I call the police."

The security chain was already in place and she was speaking to him through the small opening. Because she was so angry, she soundly closed the door and forcefully clicked the deadbolt into place.

Outraged, David banged on the door and began shouting. "Are you crazy? Who do you think you're messing with? Open this door!"

Realizing she wasn't going to open the door, David snatched his cell phone from his pocket, spun around, and headed to his car. He dialed Finell's home number. She answered right away.

"David, leave me alone. This is your last warning."

Instead of acknowledging her words, David said, "Look here, Finell. You know it's your fault that Abigail and I can't afford to make our own arrangements. You pressed charges against me for no reason at all, and now because I had to make bail and get a lawyer, we don't have any money. So it's only fair that you not cancel those arrangements. It's the least you can do, after all."

"The cancellations are a done deal!" she snapped. "Since I paid for everything out of my own pocket, I absolutely have the right to cancel them. If you'd just left me alone that Sunday and gone away, things wouldn't have happened the way they did. What happened was all *your* fault. Don't try to throw a guilt trip on me. Learn to control your temper. Have a good life." Then, just before she disconnected, she added, "Oh, and David? Don't come to my house or call me again. If you do, I'll charge you with stalking and harassment!"

David didn't want any more problems on top of the ones she'd already caused him, so instead of making her see things his way, he had his lawyer send Finell a letter the next day demanding that she return the ring.

In response, she had her lawyer send a letter informing him that since the ring had been given to her as a gift, she was allowed to retain possession of it. Then there was the fact that Finell had paid for the ring and had the receipts to prove it. Finally, David had been the one to break the contract between them. Therefore, he had forfeited ownership of the ring as well as any and all other items she'd received from him.

* * *

After tiring of her bout of unpleasant reminiscing, Finell finally threw the covers off and sat up in bed.

Well, she thought, *they've been married for almost two years now. I wonder how they liked their honeymoon.*

She let herself smile recalling that David and Abigail hadn't been able to make suitable arrangements and had ended up having a preacher marry them in the church office. Afterward, the newly married couple had spent the night in a downtown hotel.

If he'd been more sensitive to me, she thought, *maybe things would have been better for them. But at least for his sake, all he got was probation, for which he should be grateful.*

Immediately, she said aloud, "Lord, forgive me for my vindictiveness. I pray now that my heart will release this animosity and hurt I'm holding onto."

She took her Bible and her daily devotional from the nightstand and started her morning devotion. Afterward, when she stood from the bed, Finell wiped tears from her eyes. As she walked to the bathroom, she stopped in front of the mirror and looked at her reflection.

She regarded her well-proportioned, five-foot-eleven figure. She had ample breasts with deep cleavage, a defined waist, rounded hips, and a rear end you could bounce a quarter off. Below that, full muscular thighs and long, shapely legs grounded her.

Her skin was a smooth, rich nutmeg brown. Her face was exotic with naturally arched and tapered eyebrows, large almond-shaped eyes with thick lashes, and a slightly sharp nose with gently rounded nostrils—what her agent called "kissable lips." Her thick, wavy hair fell just past her shoulders like a dark-brown curtain with natural auburn highlights.

Looking like she did had helped Finell land her a job as a full-size/plus-size model when she was still in college. Being a model had helped her earn enough money to take the financial pressure off of her parents, especially when she stayed the extra year to finish the last few classes to earn her master's degree.

Finell thought about how proud her parents were when she graduated from college. Her family had shown up in full force for her special day, and they'd had a grand celebration—the first time in years they'd all had the chance to be together. Her father was just beginning his last assignment as a base commander before his official retirement from the military, and her mother was retiring from teaching. Her brother was returning from his overseas lecturing tour, and her sister had taken a week off work.

She recalled the perplexing emotion in her parents' voices when, just three years after her college graduation, she told them about her engagement to David. Then she recalled the anxiety and anger in their voices when only two years later, he left her to marry someone else.

Her parents had offered to come and comfort her, but she'd convinced them she was okay. She laughed when she thought about her brother threatening to "come into town under the veil of darkness and beat the living daylights out of that idiot!"

Her father, two-star General Alphonso Everson, reminded her that being a military brat had given her the stamina to overcome disappointments. "Young lady," he'd said in his military way, "I hope you use this opportunity to learn how to make better relationship decisions. You know how to take care of yourself and solve your own problems. Don't let that pitiful excuse for a man make you lose confidence in yourself."

Her father liked to claim he taught his children how to be across-the-board, self-sufficient, independent human beings without having to be subject to anyone for any reason. And so because of her father's convictions and warnings, she didn't let her family know she'd been plagued with nightmares about the brokenness of her life and wishful dreams about her future as a wife and mother.

Squaring her shoulders as if she were throwing off the past, she voiced her thoughts to her reflection. "You and Mom really did give us a good insight into independent living, but Daddy, you never taught me how to deal with a broken heart."

She looked in that mirror and thought, *Maybe if I had lost more than twenty-five pounds. Or maybe if I had let him make love to me just once, I would be Mrs. David Colwins right now.*

Giving a snort, she thought, *I could stand here all day and play the maybe game, but one thing is for sure. Whatever it was I did or didn't do, or said or shouldn't have said, it put an end to my relationship with David. And I'm thankful for that.*

Taking one last look at herself, she wiped her cheeks and asserted to her image, "Maybe today is the day you finally stop crying and get control of yourself, girl!" Then she turned away, went into the bathroom, and stepped into the shower.

Afterward, she refocused her thoughts before the mirror. It had been two months since her last workout session, but she'd lost another fifteen pounds. Even though the weight had come off, it hadn't been done in the proper way. She saw some changes that she didn't like and couldn't afford, especially if she was going to continue modeling.

Finell fondly recalled her college days when she'd first started modeling. She remembered how much fun it was and how happy it had made her feel. *Those were good times,* she thought. *I had lots of fun, and there was no David Colwins back then to complicate my life. But as fun as those days were, you have a real job to go to now, so get it together, girl.*

Leaving the house, Finell grabbed her workout bag. "I think you and I need to get reacquainted," she said as she slung it over her shoulder and walked out the front door.

CHAPTER 2

Joshua Hamilton closed his Bible and looked out the window of his small living room. He loved to watch the sunrise. He was grateful for the blessing to be among those who received God's promise of good health and physical strength.

Closing his eyes, Joshua offered prayers for his family members. He prayed for his decision-making abilities and all who would be affected by them. He prayed for his coworkers—especially for Finell Everson as she struggled to recover from the emotional trauma of her broken engagement.

The last prayer Joshua offered was one he offered from time to time for the spirit of forgiveness toward Marlee Turner. Often, he wondered what became of Marlee after the big argument between the Turners and Hamiltons.

Joshua and Marlee had known each other since junior high. She was a spoiled, entitled brat with rich parents who supported everything she did. Marlee was loud, outspoken, and disrespectful to the teachers. She would tease and pick on other students in her classes and dared the teachers and the principal to reprimand her for her wrongdoings. She knew her parents would go to the district superintendent and demand that anyone who disciplined their daughter be fired, as well as demanding the expulsion of any student who retaliated against her for her behavior. Mr. and Mrs. Turner were parents who overindulged their only child and were vocal against anyone who dared go against her...or them.

As an act of desperation to maintain control of her classroom, Miss Dents, the eighth-grade language arts teacher, had rearranged the seating chart and put Marlee in the empty desk beside Joshua. Miss Dents thought that since Joshua was a hardworking, quiet, focused, well-mannered young man, he would be a good influence and role model for Marlee.

Marlee liked Joshua, and because she wanted him to pay attention to her, she corralled her behavior when she was around him. Eventually, they became friends. Often during their study sessions, she would teasingly say, "When we get grown up, you're going to marry me and we're going to live happily ever after." Joshua would smile and nod his head as Marlee laughed, and they would return to their studies.

Their friendship lasted all through high school and into their junior year in college when it was discovered Marlee was pregnant and she told her parents that Joshua was the father. Mr. and Mrs. Turner demanded a meeting with the Hamiltons, insisting Joshua and Marlee marry immediately. In turn, Mr. and Mrs. Hamilton demanded a paternity test be performed, as they believed their son when he told them he was not the father.

When Joshua realized Marlee's pregnancy was the topic of their parents' discussion, he told his parents that Marlee was known at their college as a party girl who often stayed out all night and paid people to do her papers and take her tests for her. He promised his parents he hadn't had a sexual relationship with her, or anyone else, for that matter.

As a member of the Young Christians for Christ organization

on the university campus, Joshua had taken a pledge of celibacy. "The truth of the matter," Joshua told his parents, "is that I have never been sexually active. Marlee's pregnancy is not because of me."

When she first found out she was pregnant, Marlee offered Joshua money from her trust fund to say he was the father. When he refused, she claimed he'd raped her and had him arrested. When she tried to get an abortion, the Hamiltons' lawyer obtained an injunction against her and insisted the baby be placed under jurisdictional protection until its birth when the paternity test could be performed. Joshua was suspended from the university and placed under house arrest.

When the boy was born and the test results did not show conclusively that Joshua was the father, the Turners moved away overnight. Acting through their attorney, they issued an apology to the Hamiltons and offered Joshua a large settlement for the damage to his reputation. Disgustedly, Joshua refused the money. He wanted nothing to do with Marlee or her parents ever again.

This incident had been the cause of Joshua's loss of trust in the opposite sex. At the young age of nineteen, with his credibility damaged, he chose not to trust girls again. He dated when he had no choice, but he never dated a young lady more than twice—the second time usually at the request of his mother. Sometimes he dated the daughters of his mother's acquaintances, which he greatly disliked doing. Still, no amount of voicing his displeasure would deter his mother's continued attempts at setting him up.

Joshua became an introvert and limited his social life to drinking a couple of beers at the bar with his brother and his small circle of friends. Sometimes, he agreed to go on double dates with his brother. But most of Joshua's time was spent finishing his studies for his bachelor of science and MBA degrees, working his way one rung at a time up the corporate ladder of U.S. Insurances, and going to church.

Not wanting to waste any more time this morning, Joshua roused himself from his musings and finished praying. He quickly showered, dressed, and did what he did every Monday morning before leaving home: checked to see that his order was ready at the florist shop near his job, then left to pick up his tea order and get to work before anyone else arrived.

Joshua was new to the position of district manager of the northern region of U.S. Insurances, and he enjoyed it. Many employees of the district office staff were undisciplined when he arrived, and it took a lot of grit to make the necessary changes to get the productivity up to par and beyond so that the satellite offices could also be brought to standard. It was a tough two years, but he managed to get the employees to respect his changes. When they realized how successfully impacted they were by them, they gave him their trust.

Joshua realized that this acceptance had been spearheaded by Finell Everson, one of the division supervisors, who would listen to his orders and implement them in her department without question. He appreciated her for showing open-minded consideration and recognition of his authority. As a result, Finell's department was the first in the district to increase its productivity beyond its already successful performance.

Lately, thinking about Finell produced two emotional reactions in Joshua. He felt sorry that the end of her engagement had brought her so much pain and distress. And yet he was glad she hadn't gotten married because she evoked something within him that he wanted to explore.

He was attracted to her because she behaved like a lady, carried herself gracefully, was very intelligent, and had common sense. She was even-tempered and softspoken, and always dressed professionally, even on free-dress Fridays. Most of all, he found her beautiful, both with or without makeup, and being around Finell gave Joshua a sense of calm. He never felt like he had to be on guard around her.

The most amazing thing to me about that woman is her statuesque body! Joshua thought. *She's full in all the right places. Man, do I love a woman with curves!*

Before he knew it, Joshua was pulling into the employee parking lot. Despite his daydreams about Finell, he managed as always to make it to work before anyone else so he could leave his secret Monday-morning encouragements on Finell's desk without being seen.

* * *

Monday mornings at the office were still stressful for Finell, especially hearing everyone share their "I had a great weekend" stories. Once, they had included her in their conversations. But nowadays anytime she was around, the office workers quickly changed the subject or didn't speak at all. As a result, Finell had gotten into the habit of making a general greeting and walking straight to her office.

This morning, as every morning for the last year and a half, she approached her desk to find a small bowl of miniature roses, a cup of tea, an apple raisin breakfast bran muffin, and a greeting card with the day's Bible quote: *God is our refuge and our strength, a very present help in trouble* [Psalm 46:1].

The personal note that was attached read: *Keep your head up, Finell. God is always with you. Remember last week's quote? "Weeping may endure for a night, but joy comes in the morning." Your night is almost over.*

Have a blessed week. Your secret pal.

Someone had been doing that since she'd announced that her engagement had been called off. Finell wished she knew who it was so she could tell them how much she appreciated the gestures. She wanted to tell them that these acts of kindness were helping her retain her sanity.

She smiled and set the card up on her desk. Then she lifted the bowl of roses, inhaled their scent, and gently placed them on the far corner of her desk where the sun first shone in the morning. Finally, she held the cup of tea and looked out the window. The first sip, as always, was delicious.

As she stood sipping her tea, regional director Joshua Hamilton stepped into the doorway and rapped twice with his knuckle. "Miss Everson, it's eight fifty. You have five minutes to get to the weekly evaluation meeting." Then, just as quickly as he had stepped in, he left and continued to the conference room.

Finell didn't find Joshua an unfriendly man. He just didn't waste time with small talk and non-productive conversations. Simply put, Joshua Hamilton was all business, all the time. He didn't associate with any of the staff after work, and no one knew anything about his personal life. Overall, he was a good boss, and he spoke in evenly measured tones and seemed to be in control of himself at all times.

"Thank you," Finell said without turning around. She stood at the window for another two minutes. Then she turned, scooped up her folder from her desk, and left her office.

It seemed the hardest part of living through this phase of her life were the weekly evaluation meetings. Attending them forced Finell to leave her office and interact with her harshest critics, the other department leaders. Besides that, the meetings were long and boring. She couldn't understand why each of the five department heads had to present their reports to Mr. Hamilton as a group. She often wondered why he couldn't ask for the reports and read them himself, or even come around sometime during the day for a one-on-one with each of them.

In today's meeting, they were informed of a new position for a satellite office development specialist. Part of the responsibility of the position would be to travel to the region's three satellite offices once per quarter. The first assignment for the new development specialist would be to go to Parker City to conduct an on-site review of that office's medical claims records and help them clear up their backlog of insurance applications and claims.

In his direct way, Joshua told them, "This particular office has been chosen as the first to receive assistance because Parker City has the lowest production rate in the region and is in serious need of redirection. It's not going to be easy, but the new development specialist should be able to get the job done. As with all directives in this office, there's a ninety-day window for that office to show improvement or we'll be forced to take more drastic measures."

Oh wow, Finell thought. *I pity the poor person who gets the position. That sounds tough.*

Joshua saved the announcement of who was to be the development specialist for last. "Miss Everson," he said to Finell nonchalantly, "it's been decided that you are the best supervisor for the job."

At the end of the meeting, the other department supervisors congratulated Finell half-heartedly and quickly left the conference room. As soon as the others were gone, Joshua shook her hand and said, "This a very important assignment for you, Miss Everson. I want to see how well you can jump-start that office. Because after that has been straightened out, I have other things in mind that need your attention. Hopefully, you'll get the job done quickly. I've taken notice of your work ethic, and I'm very impressed."

Still holding her hand, Joshua motioned for her to take a seat. They both sat, and he continued.

"On the second and last Friday of every month, you'll be in one of the satellite offices. It seems that they're all having problems processing insurance claims within the allotted ninety-day window. Do whatever you need to do to get them up to speed. If not, we'll be forced to replace a few workers or maybe even the entire staff."

Finell was trying to focus on what her boss was saying, but it was difficult. He was still holding her hand and rubbing his thumb across the back of it. To Finell, that small gesture felt good. To have some close human contact, even if it was a simple mindless motion like this, was something she needed. It made her feel like she was worth something after all; it made her feel like something more than a reject.

When she didn't say anything, Joshua followed Finell's gaze and realized he still had possession of her hand. He lifted his eyes back to her face cleared his throat and smiled. "I'm sorry, Miss Everson. That's a habit I've developed from church." He released his hold and gently removed Finell's hand from his.

Standing quickly, Joshua put space between them by taking a seat in a chair on the opposite side of the conference table. Clearing his throat again, he lifted several sheets of paper from the table and with his eyes focused on the top sheet said, "Now, then, if you're ready, let's get started with the business at hand."

* * *

Finell and Joshua managed to fumble their way through the rest of their meeting. By the time they left the conference room, both were flustered.

She went to the ladies' room to run cold water over her hands and wrists. "Oh Lord," she said to herself in a breathy voice, "thank you for helping me to withstand the wiles of temptation. That man's hand felt so good. I've missed that kind of warmth. Actually, Lord, I don't think I've ever felt anything that mesmerizing in my life. The feel of that man's hand had me thinking about things other than work responsibilities. Help me, Lord, to hold on until you send to me the companion that you want me to have."

Joshua went to his office, walked directly to his desk, took out his Bible, and immediately turned to his favorite scripture that helped him to resist temptation: *But remember that the temptations that come into your life are no different from what others experience. And God is faithful. He will keep the temptation from becoming so strong that you can't stand up against it. When you are tempted, he will show you a way out so that you will not give in to it.* [1st Corinthians 10:13] Then he read another short scripture, Psalm 91:1: *He that dwelleth in the secret place of the most high shall abide under the shadow of the Almighty.*

"Lord," he prayed, "you know what just happened, and I want to thank you for being my rock and my shield. Thank you, Lord, for not allowing me to be taken over by lustful temptations."

* * *

It was going to be a long day for Joshua. Most of his time was going to be spent training Finell for her new job. To Joshua, the woman was pure temptation. She was not only beautiful and smelled great, but she also had a very pleasant personality.

He knew Finell was a believer because on several occasions during lunch, he had noticed her studying scripture and praying. After her engagement was abruptly ended, he sometimes saw her eating lunch alone in her office, crying and seeking God's mercy to help heal her hurt.

Witnessing that was what drove Joshua to begin leaving Finell his Monday-morning secret friend messages, hoping she would get past the pain of the betrayal and move on with her life.

"But," Joshua voiced out loud, "I need to get carnal thoughts of that woman off my mind and get back to work." Sighing, he prayed, "Lord, I need you today and every day to help me maintain my professionalism in her presence."

After lunch, Finell's phone chirped. It was Joshua.

"Miss Everson," he said, "meet me in the small conference room, and bring your laptop."

Before Finell could reply, Joshua had disconnected.

The two coworkers spent the next three hours in the conference room with the door closed and the blinds over the half-glass walls raised. They sat at opposite ends of the table. The information Joshua need to share with Finell was very descript, and he stressed how important it was that she adhere perfectly to the dictates of the rules and regulations. Looking at the thick binders, Finell knew that this and the following sessions were going to be very specific.

And as she suspected, the training sessions over the next four days were indeed intense but very educational. Finell found Joshua's deliberate and straightforward presentation enjoyable, and Joshua enjoyed it as well—especially the avidity with which the information was received. Finell's enthusiasm was, for him, a breath of fresh air.

Joshua loved seeing how Finell's eyes lit up and danced as she learned how to maximize her administrative skills. Her reception to his instruction made Josh's body have reactions he hadn't experienced in a while, and that were not appreciated in the least.

Because he wanted to wrap up training before the weekend, Joshua thought it best to stay late on Friday afternoon until they were finished. Before they both knew it, the office had closed and everyone had gone home.

At 7:15 p.m., Joshua smiled and asked, "Well, Miss Everson, how does it feel to be finished with the training?"

Finell returned his smile. "It's good to have it over with, Mr. Hamilton. Not that it was bad. But I'm going to take the weekend to review all the information so I'll be ready for my first day at the Parker City office next Friday. I'm so excited."

Joshua straightened in his chair. Inhaling deeply, he raised his hand and straightened his sagging tie. Then, after rubbing his hands together, Joshua leaned forward and pushed his chair under the table. He was feeling a little nervous about the request he was about to make.

"Well," he said haltingly, "before you go home to study, may I take you to dinner tonight?"

Suddenly Finell grew flustered. "Oh…ahh…yes, of course, It would be a good thing to go to dinner with you this evening to celebrate the end of our training sessions. That is, if you're not tired of looking at me. I'd be delighted to have dinner with you. Thank you."

Inside his chest, Joshua felt his heart skip excitedly. Smiling, he looked at his trainee and said, "Great, let's get everything shut down here and I'll follow you home, then we can go in my car and I'll bring you home afterward. So that you don't have to drive alone later tonight."

Finell thought Joshua looked even more handsome than usual. His smile seemed to light up his face. "Mr. Hamilton," she said softly, "there's no need to follow me home. Tell me where you would like to dine, and I'll meet you there." Finell hoped she didn't sound as flustered as she felt.

"Let's not have any second thoughts, Miss Everson. I wouldn't feel comfortable letting you drive home alone, especially since I was the one to suggest having dinner together anyway."

She smiled shyly and said, "Driving together is an excellent suggestion. Thank you for your kind consideration. I appreciate your thoughtfulness, even though I don't want you to have to go out of your way to take me back home later." She thought her voice sounded breathy and hoped he didn't notice.

Finell gave in to his request and gave him her address...just in case they got separated in traffic

Quickly but thoroughly shutting down the office, Joshua met Finell at the front door. After getting into their cars, Joshua followed Finell to her house. He waited in the driveway while she parked her car in the garage. Then he quickly got out, took her by the elbow, escorted her to the passenger seat, helped her in, and closed the door.

Neither Joshua nor Finell noticed the car parked across the street, or the driver that sat behind the wheel, watching them

CHAPTER 3

David Colwins watched as Finell drove her car into her garage, got out, then climbed into the passenger seat of the high-end SUV that had pulled into her driveway. He scowled with disgust as Finell and Joshua drove away. He couldn't believe what he was seeing. He was livid.

"So she's already taken up with someone," he growled. "Looks to me like she's gotten pretty chummy with that jerk, whoever he is. I'll bet she's sleeping with him." He threw his car into gear and with tires squealing drove away from Finell's home.

Dinner was a pleasant change for both Finell and Joshua. It had been a while since each had dined with someone else. The Ultimate Experience Restaurant had lived up to its name. The atmosphere was pleasant, there was a family feel to the service, the food was outstanding, and they each thought their dinner partner was entertaining and delightful.

When they arrived back at Finell's house, Joshua walked her to her door. "Thank you for sharing your evening with me," he said. "I don't think I've ever had a more pleasurable time at dinner. Have a good night."

Finell looked at her boss and couldn't help the smile that broke across her face. "It was my pleasure, Mr. Hamilton. Thank you for the invitation. Good night."

She opened her front door, and as she turned to close it, Joshua was still standing on the porch, smiling. "I'm going to stand here until I hear the lock on your door engage," he said softly, "then I'll leave."

Finell smiled then slowly closed and locked the door. She thought to herself, *I had a great time. It was nice to be with a gentleman.*

Driving to his apartment took Joshua longer than it should have. After missing his exit for the third time, he had to force himself to keep his mind on navigating the freeway traffic.

"That woman has me off my mark," he said to himself, shaking his head. "Come on, Josh. Get yourself together, man. She's not interested in you. It's too soon to make a move on her. She's still hurting from her last relationship."

Having that talk with himself didn't seem to help at all. Over the weekend, his mind kept returning to Finell. He even had recurring dreams about her. On Friday night, he had a dream about sitting beside her in church. On Saturday, he dreamed she was sitting on his lap as they ate dinner. And on Sunday morning, he found himself wishing he could look through the congregation and see her face.

Finell spent the weekend also thinking about her date with Joshua. In her mind's eye, she kept seeing the man in all of his fine, masculine appearance. Joshua stood six feet five inches tall with a slim, muscular build and long limbs. He wore his wavy hair short, which in turn accented a pleasantly handsome face dressed in a well-groomed five o'clock shadow and a manicured low-cut mustache over sensuous, well-shaped lips. Each time that vision presented itself to her, Finell had to remind herself that Joshua Hamilton was her boss and that it would not pe proper if she developed any untoward feelings for him. But that didn't mean she couldn't be nice to him and show him a token of her appreciation for his kindness toward her

When she returned to work on Monday morning, he was the first person she saw as she entered the building. When she saw him, she quickly swung her hand behind her back as he opened the door for her.

"Good Morning Miss Everson," he said. "You look very nice this morning. How was your weekend?"

Blushing Finell smiled. "Good morning back at you, Mr. Hamilton. I had a wonderful weekend. Thanks to you."

They stood smiling at each other like two people who shared a secret until Finell remembered what she had hidden behind her back.

"Oh, I'm sorry," she said, "these are for you." Finell swung her arm back around and presented her boss with a bouquet of brightly colored wildflowers.

"Wow. Aren't these beautiful?" Joshua exclaimed. "Thank you. What are they for?"

"I just wanted to let you know that I enjoyed dinner on Friday. And rather than write a thank-you card, especially since I don't know your address, I decided to bring you some flowers."

"Well, thank you. They are very nice. This is the first time anyone has ever given me flowers. And I think I like it." Joshua raised the bouquet to his nose and inhaled. Then he took her arm and said, "What do you say we go get these in some water?"

Finell managed to make it through the rest of the day without marching into her boss's office, grabbing him by his lapels, pulling him close, and kissing him until she was breathless. She did so by praying for strength and clarity of mind every time they were in the same space together. It was a highly stressful day. Not because of the work but because of Joshua and her growing affinity for the man.

That night after work, Finell walked into her house and kicked off her shoes. "Oh, thank you, Jesus," she said.

For the last year and a half, she'd felt that if she made it through Monday without a meltdown, the rest of the week would be stress-free. But now that she was at home within the walls of 1977 Laramore Drive, she could let her mind settle all it wanted on whatever or whomever she wanted. Tonight, it seemed her mind was going to settle on the USI regional offices director.

"Now, that Joshua Hamilton," she said out loud to herself, "is one truly good-looking man. If he wasn't the boss, I wouldn't have to think twice about getting to know him a little better. Because that man is really, without any objection, just plain *fine*!" She laughed out loud at her declaration of admiration for her boss.

Finell stood in her entryway, still holding onto the doorknob to her front door, looking around the furnished reception area that served as her downtime room. On the long wall was a pair of Queen Anne high-back recliners with a small music entertainment system in a narrow tower between them. On the short wall across the entry hall was a five-foot bookcase with etched beveled glass doors.

Still smiling, she admitted to herself, "There hasn't been that kind of emotion in this place in a long while. It feels good."

She checked the front door, securing the lock and chain, then took off her coat and hung it on the coat tree between the bookcase and the table. She put her cell phone on its charger and slid her purse into the drawer. The final part of her routine was to put her keys in the small basket on the tabletop.

This was usually the time when tears would spill from her eyes and she would spend the rest of her evening feeling sorry for herself. But on this particular evening, Finell felt she was finally free from the shame and embarrassment of having been jilted.

All it had taken to get her here was a dinner with Joshua Hamilton.

I know it was three days ago and that it was probably nothing to him. But it meant the world to me, she happily acknowledged to herself.

Suddenly, Finell remembered her Monday-morning bowl of roses was still in her car, which she's also forgotten to park in the garage. Snatching up her keys, she walked quickly to her front door. When she opened it, she let out a scream.

* * *

Finell tried to close her front door, but David stuck his foot in the jamb.

"What are you doing here?" she snapped, leaning her weight against the door.

"You still have something that belongs to me, and I want it back!" David demanded.

"I don't have anything that belongs to you," Finell said, addressing him with a tone of tired finality. "Our lawyers already settled everything! Besides, that ring is no more anyway. I had a necklace made from the stones. Now, get away from my house!"

"I'm not leaving until I get what I came for, or a reasonable substitution," David snarled.

"Go away, David! Leave me alone, or I'm going to call the police." Finell tried pushing the door closed, but by this time David was leaning his weight against it.

"Go ahead, Finell, make that call. By the time they get here, I will have gotten what I came for and I'll be gone."

Just as she was losing the battle, a voice in the dark said, "Is there a problem here? Do you need some help, Miss Everson?"

Turning his head, David regarded the well-dressed stranger standing at the end of the walkway. "Beat it," he said, "this doesn't concern you."

David gave the door one final push, knocking Finell backward and sending her down against the third step of her staircase.

As the stranger advanced on him, David launched into a volley of insults that he didn't finish. "This is between me and this thieving, fat bit—" he began, but suddenly found himself on the ground holding his mouth.

"No one disrespects a woman in my presence, especially this woman," Joshua said. "I think you should get up and leave!"

David rose unsteadily to his feet with the intent of hitting back, but he thought better of it when he noticed the disparity in their sizes. At six-foot-one, David felt short in comparison.

"I've seen you before," David said. "You're her new stud, aren't you?" He swung around and glared at Finell. "You'd sleep with him but not me, huh? Is he the reason you froze me out?" Wiping his bloodied mouth with his coat sleeve, David walked across the lawn to his car parked at the curb. Before he drove away, he called, "This isn't over, Finell!"

Giving Joshua a look of surprise, Finell smiled sadly and with an unsteady voice said, "Thank you, Mr. Hamilton. I appreciate your help."

"No problem, Miss Everson. Looks like I was just in time."

Joshua stepped through the doorway and offered her his hand. Standing, Finell straightened her dress and closed the front door. "Let me have your coat," she said. "Feel free to take a seat. I'm going to get you some ice for your hand."

She gestured toward the chairs in her reception area and tried discreetly to rub some of the pain from her rear end as she walked into her kitchen.

When she returned, Finell asked, "What brings you here this evening, Mr. Hamilton?" to which Joshua immediately asked himself, *Yes, Joshua, what are you doing here?*

Finell handed him a cold-pack compress and Joshua took it, resting it on his sore knuckles. Seeing that she was expecting an answer to her question, he cleared his throat and said, " I was trying to catch you before you reached your car after work this evening. When I was leaving the building, I noticed that guy sitting in his car in the parking lot and realized he was focused on you. So, when he started following you, I decided to follow him. And when I saw he was not a friendly person, I thought I would offer my services."

"I'm so grateful that you were here to help," Finell said.

The two colleagues stood for a few moments in silence, looking at each other, both liking very much what they were seeing.

Finell caught herself staring into Joshua's eyes. They were almost entirely black but were offset by golden flecks, and they were presently focused on Finell's hand, which was rubbing her sore hip. She let her eyes roam down to his lips, unconsciously licking her own.

Joshua caught himself looking into Finell's exotic brown eyes. Hers was the most beautiful face he had ever seen. She had a creamy smooth complexion and a sculpted face with high cheekbones, a rounded chin, and full, moist lips. His eyes again moved from her face to the hand on her hip, then slowly back up to her face by way of her breasts, shoulders, and neck.

To break the silence and reset his mind, Joshua said, "If you don't mind my asking, who is that guy? Do we need to call the police?"

"Do you want the long version or the short one?" she asked, smiling sadly. Before he could answer, Finell motioned for him to take a seat. "That's David Colwins, my former fiancé. He was here demanding that I give him the ring I wore while we were engaged."

"Really? Why does he want that ring so badly?"

"He wants to give it to his wife. He claims that because I had him arrested and pressed charges against him, he couldn't afford a decent ring for her. He insists that since we didn't get married, he should get it back."

Joshua scratched his chin. "If you don't mind my asking, Miss Everson, do you still have feelings for him?"

"Heavens, no!" Finell exclaimed. "Why would you ask me something like that?"

"Because I would think that you'd want to get rid of everything and anything that reminds you of him."

"If you must know," Finell said, "I kept the ring because I paid for it. All except for the $150 down payment he made. As a matter of fact, I paid for everything related to our ill-fated wedding."

"How did that happen?"

"Well, he would initiate purchases like our honeymoon package, the flowers, the cake, and the reception hall. He would make the minimal necessary deposits. Then afterward, he would tell me I should go ahead and pay for it because I have a higher credit card limit. He said he would repay me in cash just before we got married."

"So, is this the first time that he has accosted you?" Joshua asked.

"This isn't the first time he's asked for the ring, if that's what you mean," Finell said, filling Joshua in on all the details of David's unreasonable demands. "He's called me twice since they've been married. He says he wants us to get together for lunch and talk over old times and clear the air between us."

When Josh didn't comment, Finell felt compelled to go on. "I know it sounds ridiculous. I feel like such a fool. I should have been able to recognize the flaws in his personality, but I think I was so caught up in the idea of getting married that I didn't stop to think about the absurdity of the whole situation. I know now that he didn't love me. He was just using me, and I think that coming to terms with that was what hurt the most. It wasn't the fact that he dumped me to marry someone else. It was how he did it. I think I knew all along, in the back of my mind, that we weren't going to get married. I just didn't want to admit it to myself."

They sat together for a while longer and had a cup of tea and some homemade tea cookies. Then Joshua left, wishing Finell a good night and reminding her that he was going to be away at a convention for the next three days.

"Hold down the fort for me, Miss Everson, and I'll hopefully see you on Thursday afternoon."

CHAPTER 4

It was Friday morning. Finell was fifteen miles into her forty-five-mile drive to Parker City when her cell phone rang. Pressing the answer button on her steering wheel, she answered.

It was Joshua. "Miss Everson, have you left for Parker City yet?"

"Good morning, Mr. Hamilton, welcome back. I'm fifteen miles into the drive. What can I do for you?"

Joshua's voice was filled with a smile. "I wanted to let you know that I'm going to meet you there this afternoon."

Finell's face lit up. "Why? Don't you trust your training skills, Mr. Hamilton?"

She heard him chuckle. "I'm going to be there just to offer some moral support, so you won't be nervous, since this is your first assignment. And I promise you that you'll be totally on your own the next time."

"Well, thank you for the support. And I'll be glad to see you," she added, a smile in her voice as well.

"Goodbye, Miss Everson," Joshua said slowly.

Although she wasn't ready to end their conversation, Finell said, "Goodbye, Mr. Hamilton."

Finell was smiling pleasantly when she arrived at the Parker City satellite office of U.S. Insurances. She was twenty minutes early and had to wait outside with several staff members for the doors to be unlocked, but she had a feeling her presence was not appreciated. The staff workers looked at her but no one returned her smile.

After finally arriving and opening the doors, the office manager, Devin Martin, responded to Finell's self-introduction in a drab, deadpan voice. "Well, now, I wasn't expecting you so early, but since you're here, we may as well get this thing started. Let me show you to the conference room."

Finell took in the man's attitude—as well as his no handshake, no offer of coffee, and scowl-and-grunt greeting—as a sign that things might not go very well.

Undaunted by the fear of the staff members and the rudeness of their boss, Finell began her presentation and training session. The first thing she did was assure the staff that she was there to show them how to improve their office productivity and not to eliminate jobs.

From that point, she saw shoulders relax, heard sighs of relief, and felt the atmosphere become lighter. It became easy to disseminate the information once the air was cleared.

Still, the office manager did not become any more friendly. Each time Finell looked at him during her presentation, Devin Martin's face was drawn and tight-lipped. His body language was defensive, and his attitude was wholly unprofessional.

By the time Joshua arrived at the Parker City office, Finell was ending the slideshow presentation that served as the first phase of the retraining process.

Joshua looked around and saw that the office workers seemed appreciative of the attention they were receiving.

Finell addressed the employees. "So, ladies and gentlemen, what I would like for you to do now is to return to your workstations, take out all of your case folders, and begin to check and upload all of the basic information for each case on your computers. Then check the status of each claim. I'm sure that by the end of today, you'll have discovered that you're further ahead on your cases than you think."

Looks of relief and renewed determination reflected on the faces of the staff. Joshua realized that Finell had done a good job of getting them on her side and helping them understand they were valuable to the success of the company. Finell looked at Joshua, nodded her head, then left the conference room to walk around the office and offer support to the staff.

Devin Martin was sitting at the end of the conference table with his arms folded across his chest, looking very put out. When he saw Joshua come into the room, he almost ran over to him.

"Good afternoon, Mr. Hamilton," Devin said. "May I have a word with you, please?" After the two men walked into his office, Devin asked, "How often is she going to be here? I don't like her. She's pushy and aggressive. And she's been encouraging my people to go against all of my office rules."

Joshua was surprised. "Just what is it that she's saying to the staff that you don't agree with, Mr. Martin?"

Devin's reply sounded agitated. "For one thing, she told them they should take a ten-minute break every hour just to refresh themselves. Then she said she didn't have a problem with them listening to music at their workstations as long as it doesn't disturb their neighbors and slow productivity. And she suggested to them that every Monday at the weekly staff meeting they should set a quota of cases they each want to have completed by the end of each week. I think she's simply overstepped her boundary. She needs to leave here and not come back."

"I'm still waiting for you to tell me something I disagree with," Joshua said. "So please, tell me. What is the problem?"

"She came in here and started questioning me!" Devin said. "Like I was the one who needed to be put in my place. Then she asked to see my staff's performance records, and when I told her they weren't up to date, she insisted I get them done so she can review them before she leaves this afternoon. Then right in the staff meeting, she threw me under the bus. She said I should be considered the last previewer of all the cases processed daily. She contends that no case is settled or complete until I've read the file and initialed the final paperwork."

"Listen to me Mr. Martin," Joshua said, "it sounds like Miss Everson is right on the mark with everything that has been done here today. You do realize that she's here to help this office to improve its productivity, don't you?"

Devin Martin looked at Joshua and sneered, "Well, we don't need her here to tell us what to do. I was getting everything back under control myself."

Joshua stood. "Just so we're clear. You would be doing yourself a favor if you remember that she's just doing her job. And if I were you, I would begin to implement her suggestions as soon as possible. That is, if you want to keep your job."

"Well, I don't want her here," Devin went on. "She's not respecting me. She needs to go, and I don't want her to ever come back! I can work with you better than I want to with her."

Joshua leaned in and spoke in a low, even voice. "Mr. Martin, let me suggest that you rethink your request. It may not be a good thing for you. Miss Everson is here to analyze the entire office procedure from top to bottom. Just one word from her and you could be out of a job. Think about this for just a bit. Why don't we wait a month to see if things begin to improve around here before you make any waves?"

* * *

Finell saw the two men talking, and it didn't seem to be a friendly exchange. She could see Devin Martin's face as he talked to Joshua, and Devin didn't appear to be in the least bit pleased with what he was being told.

She knew Devin wasn't in favor of her presence by the way he greeted her when she first arrived. When Joshua left the administrative office, Finell looked for signs of displeasure or anger, but he looked his usual calm, unflappable self.

She turned back to the staff member she was helping as Joshua walked up behind her and said, "I hope you can wrap it up here in enough time to get back to the office before five o'clock, Miss Everson. We have some matters to discuss." Then, without waiting for a response, he walked out of the building, got into his car, and drove away.

The staff member, a young lady in her twenties, looked at Finell. "Wow! What was that about? Is he always like that? I certainly hope not. Brother is *way* too fine to come across so stoic and inflexible all the time."

Finell smiled. "Oh, he's...umm...he's a good boss. It's just that he's a very focused person. He doesn't step outside of professional protocol too often."

The young lady gave Finell an amused look. "Oh, okay. Whatever you say, my sister!" Then she smiled. "How 'bout we get this done so you can get on the road? I wouldn't want you to be late getting back to your office. We wouldn't want your boss to blow a gasket."

Both ladies giggled and returned to work.

It was just after two o'clock when the last workers returned from lunch. Finell reviewed some of the errors she found were being made most often and showed the staff how to avoid making them again. Then she left with a promise to return before the end of the quarter.

It was quarter to five when Finell returned to the main office. Most everyone was gone, so she went directly to her office, filled out her evaluation sheets and her mileage report, then walked quickly to Joshua's office and knocked.

"Come in," he called out. "Oh, Miss Everson, you're back. How did things go after I left?"

"Things went just fine, Mr. Hamilton. Thank you for your support. I don't think that Mr. Martin likes me very much."

Joshua's eyebrows lifted. "Why would you say something like that?" He sounded anxious. "Did you have a conversation with him after I left?"

"No, we didn't talk after our initial conversation, which was rather curt. I can't say anything other than when I first arrived, he wasn't very friendly or helpful. And he didn't seem to want my input on anything." A quizzical look broke across her face. "Why do you ask? Did he say something to you?"

Looking at Finell for a long moment, Joshua cleared his throat. "Let's just say that he and I had a conversation. My suggestion to him was that he follow your directives and the office will begin to meet corporate expectations. If that happens, then he may not face the threat of losing his job."

"Oh. And did he take your advice?"

"Well, we'll see in a month from now when we review his staff's productivity and performance rates."

The two stood looking at each other for a few moments.

She is so beautiful, Joshua thought. *How could anyone not want to spend the rest of their life with her?*

Meanwhile, Finell was lost in her own thoughts. *He's such a gentleman. Why isn't he married? There must be some kind of hidden flaw. I wonder what it is.*

Finell was the first to break the extended eye contact. "I forgot to welcome you back, Mr. Hamilton. And I want to thank you again for your support this morning. I hope you have a restful weekend."

"Well, thank you, Miss Everson," Joshua said with a smile. "You're quite welcome. I hope you have a good weekend also. Goodnight."

When Finell turned to leave his office, Joshua quickly called her back.

"Oh, one more thing, Miss Everson. Would you…would you like to…have lunch with me after church on Sunday?"

With a modest smile, Finell said, "That would be nice. But we'll have to make it another day. I'll be out of the office until next Thursday. When I spoke with the HR director, he assured me that you would receive a memo about my leave. I'm a seasonal model, and it's time to begin working on next season's catalog. Let's talk when I return so we can set the date."

Smiling, Joshua nodded his head slowly. "Will do, Miss Everson."

Joshua was glad Finell left his office door open when she left. He truly enjoyed watching her walk away.

CHAPTER 5

The following morning, Finell snapped the airplane seatbelt across her hips, leaned back against the headrest, and closed her eyes. She smiled when she thought about how her boss—the very stoic, deliberate, unattached, and very handsome Joshua Hamilton—had asked her out. She knew it probably wouldn't be an official date, but she was still excited about anything within reason that would help her get past the memories of her previous nightmare-invoking relationship.

To her, Joshua emanated a quiet strength. And although he wielded his authority unyieldingly, he was kind. He had a soft smile which he didn't display often, but when he did smile, it was smooth and genuine. He had a fluid walk, and his stance was straight and attention-grabbing. If he wasn't such a gentleman, he could charm a woman right out of her shoes and her better judgment.

For the second time in as many days, Finell wondered, *Why isn't he married?* Then, realizing where her mind was going, she hunched her shoulders and declared, *Who cares? I'm not trying to be in a relationship. The man just asked me to lunch after church. It's not like he's asking me to be his woman.*

Finell's eyes flew open, slightly disgusted with herself for her train of thought, so she snatched her book out of her bag and began to read, hoping it would get her mind off Joshua.

Finell is a seasonal and holiday catalog model. She enjoyed modeling but chose not to continue with it as a full-time career after college. It was a hectic life that was filled with lots of highs and lows. It was challenging for many of the men and women who modeled for a living, the hours were unpredictable, the pace was hectic, and for a field that required lots of discipline, many of the models were far from being very self-disciplined. Many of them led a wild no holds barred existence and Finell didn't care for a lifestyle that was so recklessly impulsive.

With Finell out of town and unable to meet him after church, Joshua was forced to have Sunday afternoon lunch with his family. First, he attended the Good Samaritan Church's 8:00 a.m. service. Then he taught church school and officiated over the eleven o'clock praise and worship portion of the service. Finally, he presented the pulpit devotion and gave the benediction. Afterward, he met his family downtown at the Hamilton Suites Grand Hotel restaurant.

Myra Hamilton, his mother, was overjoyed to see her baby boy walk into the restaurant. "Oh, hello darling. I'm glad to see you. Come give Mommy a kiss and a hug."

Edwin Hamilton Sr. looked at Joshua with no greeting and said, "So, to what do we owe the honor of your presence this afternoon? It's been a while since you had lunch with us."

Before Joshua could answer, his older brother, Edwin Jr., said, "Hey, Josh, glad to see you, man. Come sit here." He pointed to the seat next to him. "So what have you been up to?"

Edwin Jr. didn't want to have anything to do with the family's insurance and hotel ownership business, but he respected his younger brother's efforts to be involved. Edwin Jr. was a pilot who owned his own private airport and a fleet of commuter planes. His business was thriving, and he had no intention of ever working for his father. Being too much alike, they hardly ever got along.

In his private heart, Edwin Jr. thought Joshua was a wimp for letting their father treat him like one of the servants and not insisting that their mother treat him like an adult instead of a dim-witted teenager. And yet Edwin Jr. did all he could to act as a buffer between his parents and his younger brother. After all, wasn't that what big brothers were supposed to do?

The Hamilton family mealtime session was long, and for Joshua, it was intense. His father used the time to ask questions about the office, in particular why he was making the changes he was making. Edwin Sr. also spent a good amount of time telling Joshua about the complaint registered against him by Devin Martin.

"So just who is this woman that you sent to his office to embarrass him and challenge his authority?" he asked.

Closing his eyes momentarily, Joshua offered, "Dad, Miss Everson is a good employee. If you remember, when I first took over as regional director, her division was the only one that met and even exceeded corporate expectations. All she did was go to Devin's satellite office, retrain the workers, and reset some general office rules. And as you also know, Miss Everson's division at the regional offices always has a rating that is seventy-five percent above the other division supervisors. That's why she was chosen as the new development specialist."

"That may be all well and good," Joshua's father said, "but you should have known better than to send a woman to do that job. Who is she, anyway? What do you know about her?"

Suppressing a huff and eye roll, Joshua said, "Her name is Finell Everson, and she's very good at her job. I knew we weren't using her to her fullest potential by keeping her in the office. And after observing her in the field, I realized I was right. She has a strong work ethic. She gets along well with people, has a wealth of knowledge, and she's creative. Because of all that, I think she's a valuable asset in the company's growth. She's a real asset to USI."

Edwin Jr. looked at his brother with surprise. "Did you say Finell Everson?"

"Yeah. Why?"

"Why? Man, that woman is *hella* fine. I just flew her and the rest of her crew to Palm Springs. She's a model. As a matter of fact, she's one of her agent's premier models. Finell Everson has a good name among the major catalog companies and clothes designers. Damn, man, you know Finell! Have you tapped that thang yet?"

Feeling heat flash throughout his body, Joshua turned to look at his brother. "EJ," he said, calling his brother by his nickname, "it's not like that, man. She's a lady. You don't treat ladies like sex objects."

"Oh, come on man, the woman's a model. I'll bet she's a freak. You need to freak that."

"Ed, come on! She's a real lady *and* a good employee. She's not like that. Just knock it off."

"Oh, yeah, I forgot," Edwin Jr. said, clapping Joshua on the back. "You're still a virgin. Waiting for God to send you a wife. Well, keep on waiting, little brother. And in the meantime, you're missing out on a good thing. If her agent didn't have a contract with EHJ Flights, I'd make my move. I'd have my face buried between those fleshy mountains on her chest, my hands would be full of that voluptuous heart-shaped bottom, and her firm thighs would be wrapped around my hips!"

"Watch your mouth, boy," Edwin Sr. said. "You know better than to talk like that around your mother." Even though he was admonishing his son, there was a grin on his face.

Joshua punched his brother on the shoulder. "Stop! You're a real jerk. I don't deny she's a beautiful woman, but I refuse to treat her like a sex object. She's just getting over a bad break-up. Her fiancé jilted her. The last thing she needs right now is somebody making moves on her."

"Good for you," Mrs. Hamilton said. "Just keep waiting for God to bless you with the right woman. A godly marriage is a happy marriage." She sent her husband a guarded look, then continued. "I don't blame you for being cautious, Joshy. I wouldn't think that a model would have the proper breeding to be your wife."

"Yeah, whatever," Edwin Sr. said. Then, turning to Joshua, he added, "Boy, you need to get you some good loving from a beautiful woman every once in a while. Maybe you wouldn't be so uptight all the time." He laughed heartily with a gleam in his eye. "Sex is a good stress reliever. You ought to try it sometime. You know, it only takes once and you're hooked."

* * *

Joshua stood from the lunch table and kissed his mother. "Love you, Mom." Then he shook hands with his father. "Goodbye, Dad."

When he hugged his brother, Edwin Jr. winked. "Thanks for getting him started, and for the mental pictures. You're my personal porno pimp."

The brothers laughed, released each other from their hug, and fist-bumped.

As he drove home, Joshua fought to keep the images Edwin Jr. had painted of Finell out of his mind. It seemed his brother's words had only increased his interest in Finell. Later that evening, Joshua finally stopped fighting himself and let his thoughts drift back to his brother's comments concerning Finell Everson as her modeling agent's premier client. *Seems that Miss Everson's work ethic is applied to every aspect of her life,* he thought.

It wasn't a stretch for Joshua to imagine Finell standing before a camera posing in outfits that she made look amazing. For the rest of the night, Joshua had visuals in his mind about her that vacillated between her modeling signature outfits to the sexual scenes invoked by his brother's crude comments.

It made sense that she was a model. At five feet eleven inches, Finell was a stunning woman. It had not gotten past him that she was classically beautiful. Her hair was a natural dark mahogany brown with dark auburn highlights that flashed in the sunlight as it filtered through the window blinds behind her desk.

Every time he let himself look at her, he noticed her complexion was creamy smooth, even, and unblemished, while her soft, perfectly formed and inviting lips begged him to taste them for their hidden sweetness. She was a full-sized woman with curves that made a real man want to cross the line of propriety and test her rigid state of modesty.

From the first time he saw her, Finell Everson made Joshua Hamilton begin to think not all women were like his mother and Marlee Turner. Realizing that he was losing sleep thinking about her, Joshua said a prayer for Finell and then recited scripture until he drifted off into a dreamless rest.

* * *

It was early Thursday morning, and Finell was not feeling well. Her stomach was unsettled, her head and all of her joints ached, and she was so tired she could hardly walk. Along with that, she felt hot all over. She couldn't wait to get home.

The modeling session had been a long one. Most of it had been spent on the beach in bathing suits from sunup to sundown. She was sure she was suffering from overexposure to the sun.

She spent most of the day Thursday in airports and getting off and back onto the plane. The pilot had to make four stops, which translated to a long day of traveling. All she wanted to do was get home, take a warm bath, put on her pajamas, crawl into bed, and sleep until she was feeling better. As soon as she got home that night, Finell called in sick to work for Friday and prepared to spend the rest of the weekend in bed.

Joshua was disappointed when he found out from Finell's assistant that she wasn't coming in. He had been looking forward to seeing her all week, and now he'd have to wait for Monday. As disappointed as he was, he was sorry to hear she wasn't feeling well.

By lunchtime, he realized that he had to see her, so he mentally put a plan in place that would ensure connecting with Finell. After a few calls, Joshua gave himself a mental shake and returned his focus to the work sitting on his desk that needed his attention.

He planned on going to see Finell after work, but when he got to his home, his mother ambushed him with Petra Raymond. Petra was the daughter of a deacon at their church. Joshua didn't care for Petra; she was too forward, and because of that, he tried to stay as far away from her as he possibly could. His trepidations concerning Petra were that she was a touchy-feely person and had been trying to create opportunities to sleep with him for years.

When he pulled into his apartment building's assigned parking space, Joshua saw his mother's car parked in the visitor's slot next to his. She was sitting behind the wheel, Petra Raymond sitting proudly beside her.

NIGHTMARE

"Hello, son," Myra Hamilton said, stepping out of her car. Petra followed her, and they both approached Joshua. "Petra and I were out shopping today, and she asked me about you. Imagine my surprise when she told me you hadn't seen each other since she returned home. I thought maybe you and she could have dinner together tonight."

Not wanting to cause a scene and hurt Petra's feelings, Joshua kept a pleasant expression on his face and said, "Mom, I kinda had plans for tonight."

"Oh? Well, surely you can change them, can't you? After all, Petra is already here, and I have to get home to meet your dad. We have a dinner date tonight also. Oh, I've just had the most marvelous idea! Why don't you and Petra meet us at the Grand Hotel? We'll be there at seven. See you then."

Without another word, Myra jumped back into her car and drove off, leaving Petra and Joshua staring at each other.

It took all the patience Joshua had to spend the evening with Petra and his parents. He was livid. His mother had set him up. And with a woman who must have had eight arms. He spent most of the night sliding her hands off almost every part of his body.

For years, Myra Hamilton had been throwing women in her son's face. He had told her more than a few times that he didn't appreciate it, but it seemed his protests fell on deaf ears. At least once a month, his mother introduced him to someone and tried to set them up on a date. For the most part, the dates weren't bad. They ran the gamut from quiet, mousy girls to snobbish and self-centered women, to those who were desperate to be married and thought any man would do. But tonight, he had reached his limit. He was definitely going to tell her, "No more!"

By nine thirty that evening, Joshua was too angry to talk. He was sick of Petra. And now he had finally arrived at the house where she was living. They were parked at the curb outside her parents' house when she reached across the seat and touched high up on his inner thigh...again.

Joshua quickly grabbed her hand and cringed. Petra said, "We don't have to call it a night just yet, you know. I want to show you my appreciation for dinner."

Still holding her hand, Joshua tried to hide his anger. "Maybe some other time, Petra. I had a long day at work, and I'm really tired."

Petra looked startled. "Too tired for all of this?" she said and waved her other hand over her body as she lifted her chest and shook her shoulders, aiming her breasts in his direction.

Trying not to let his displeasure show in his voice, Joshua said, "Well, I would suppose for some, that's a real...temptation. But I'm extremely tired. I wouldn't be at my best tonight. I'd hate to cheat you. Good night, Petra." Then he bolted from the car, ran around to the passenger side, and just about snatched the door open.

As Joshua walked Petra to her front door, she grabbed a handful of his rear end. "I can't imagine you not being at your best. You're in great shape. I can tell you take care of your body. You look smoking hot. I'd like to be part of your regular workout regimen."

Grabbing her hand, he held onto it until they reached the porch steps. He let her walk up to the porch landing while he stood at the base of the steps. As soon as her foot landed on the porch, the front door swung open and Deacon Raymond stepped out.

"Good evening, young man. That was quite a long dinner date. I hope you behaved like a gentleman."

"Yes he did, Daddy," Petra said. "Mr. Hamilton was a true gentleman tonight. We had dinner with his parents. Then I asked him to walk me through the square downtown so I could see the changes that have happened since I've been away." She turned to Joshua. "I appreciate a man with good manners. I hope we can do this again, Mr. Hamilton."

Petra walked down two steps, leaned forward, kissed Joshua on the cheek (because he quickly turned his head), and said, "Good night. Don't forget you promised to call me."

Joshua turned and walked back to his car. As he drove away, he mumbled to himself, "I'll call you when hell freezes over." The sigh that he released sounded more like a growl.

* * *

Saturday was a busy day for Joshua. He had a meeting with the church's youth committee as well as a meeting with the pastor concerning his duties as the church's newly appointed Bible study director. By the time he got home, it was four thirty and he thought it was too late to visit Finell, so he called her.

"Hello?" she answered, her voice sleepy and sexy.

"Miss Everson, this is Joshua Hamilton. I'm calling to ask how you are feeling."

"Oh, Mr. Hamilton." Finell's voice perked up, and Joshua could sense her smiling. "Thank you for calling me. I'm feeling better today. How did you know I was sick?"

"Martina, the HR assistant, told our secretary, Mrs. Mimms, who in turn told me. So, Miss Everson…if you remember, just before you left, I asked you to have Sunday lunch with me."

"Mr. Hamilton, I would be glad to have lunch with you next Sunday. I know I'll be feeling so much better by then. Thank you for calling. I hope you have a good night."

"Good night, Miss Everson. Get better." Then, as he was

hanging up the phone, Joshua thought, *There's no way I'm going to wait another whole week to spend time with you, woman. I'm going to see you tomorrow!*

After church on Sunday afternoon, Joshua stopped by the Gardens of Love restaurant and picked up four quarts of soup: chicken noodle, minestrone, lobster bisque, and hardy garden vegetable. He didn't know what Finell liked, so he got his favorites and hoped she would appreciate at least one of them.

He honestly didn't care if she didn't like any of the choices. If she didn't, he'd gladly go somewhere else and get whatever she wanted. His desire to have an excuse just to see her on a personal basis was strong.

Joshua rang the doorbell, but after two or three minutes, he was still standing waiting for Finell to open the door. He rang again and was surprised when she opened the door in a caftan that clung to her body enough to let him know there was nothing underneath. Her feet were bare, her face was free of makeup, and her hair was wrapped in a towel.

Holding the bag in front of himself, Joshua stammered, "M-Miss Everson...Uh, I brought you some lunch. Is...is this a bad time?" He was struggling to keep his eyes on her face.

Finell stepped behind the door. "Mr. Hamilton, good afternoon. I'm just getting out of the tub, so I'm going to have to run back upstairs. But you should come in and close the door." When he hesitated, she repeated, "Come on in. I'll be right back."

Stepping inside the house, he watched as Finell ran back up the steps, giving him a view of her rear end outlined by that clinging caftan. And indeed, it was just as his brother had said: a well-rounded, very firm, upside-down heart-shaped work of art.

"Damn," Joshua said under his breath quickly, moving his eyes down to the toe of his shoe, and shook his head. "Lord, forgive me for my moment of weakness."

"What was that?" Finell called down to him. "I didn't understand what you said."

"*Down*," he said, speaking loudly enough for her to hear. "I need to put these bags *down*."

"Oh. The kitchen is to your right, down the hall just past the dining room. Make yourself at home. I'll be right with you."

In the kitchen, Joshua put the bags on the counter and began to unpack them. He washed his hands and looked through the cabinets, taking down bowls for the soup, bread plates for the rolls, and glasses for drinks.

When she stepped into the kitchen, Finell had on a pair of jeans and a swing-top blouse. "Well, what do we have here? And to what do I owe the pleasure of your company?"

"If you can remember, it was today that we were supposed to have lunch together after church. So when I heard you weren't feeling well, I decided to bring you some soup. Mrs. Wilson always made soup for me when I was sick. She says it's a natural cure for whatever ails you."

Smiling, Finell asked, "Is Mrs. Wilson your mother?"

"No," Joshua said, frowning. "Mrs. Wilson was our nanny."

"Oh," Finell said, somewhat surprised. She felt the atmosphere in the room shift, so she changed the subject. "What kind of soup do we have?"

"I didn't know what you liked, so I have some of my favorites. I hope you like them." He told her what he bought, his voice perking up as he did.

"I like soup," Finell said, "so let's taste them all."

They sat at the kitchen table and sampled the contents of each container. His favorite was the minestrone; hers was the lobster bisque. To go along with the soups, Finell used the rolls he brought and made small grilled cheese sandwiches. Then she served chilled homemade peach tea.

"I didn't know that you're a model," Joshua said. "How long have you been doing that?"

Finell told him she did runway modeling to get through college and answered his questions about why she toned down her career, especially why she preferred working at USI rather than being a full-time model.

It was six o'clock in the evening by the time Joshua left Finell's house. They had eaten, cleaned the kitchen, gone through some of the professional photographs from her career photo collections, and watched the early evening news.

As they stood at the front door, Finell put out her hand. "Thank you for your company today, Mr. Hamilton. It was very uplifting for me to have dinner with you."

Joshua took her hand and stepped close. "It was my pleasure. And I'm Joshua. I'm only Mr. Hamilton at work." Looking down at her, he smiled and kissed her cheek. "Good night, Finell."

As she closed the door, Finell whispered to herself, "Oh, my goodness. That man is *fine*!" She leaned her back against the closed door and with the tips of her fingers she lightly touched her cheek where his lips had been. Closing her eyes, she sighed and smiled broadly.

* * *

By Monday morning, Finell was feeling much better. Her body wasn't aching, and she was well rested. She realized that she was feeling happier than she had in more than two years. And she attributed it to one person and his simple act of kindness. An act of kindness that helped her get a full night's sleep, something that had eluded her since before her broken engagement.

When she arrived at work, she was excited to see Joshua. After spending the previous day with him, she wanted to see him and thank him again for his kindness. As always, on Monday mornings there was her usual secret friend offering. Today, the theme focused on forgiveness; she thought that her secret friend seemed to be able to look inside of her and touch those tender spots in her heart.

The note began with a Bible verse from Matthew 6:14: *"For if you forgive others their trespasses, your heavenly Father will also forgive you."*

Underneath that were these words: *Just remember, Finell, if you don't allow your heart to heal from your last relationship, your next relationship will be doomed. If you want to heal your broken heart, maybe Psalm 55:22 can help you. It says "Cast your burden on the Lord, and He will sustain you; He will never permit the righteous to be moved." God bless you, your secret pal.*

The tea was still hot, and the apple raisin walnut muffin was still warm. Finell knew she had just missed whomever it was who was being so nice to her. She suspected that it could be Mrs. Mimms, their secretary. Mrs. Mimms was the only office worker who had shown her any sympathy when David ended their engagement.

Finell remembered how the sweet older woman had quietly walked into her office several times to find her crying. Rather than ridicule her, Mrs. Mimms comforted her and assured her that everything would be alright. "You just go ahead and cry, little girl, but not too long. It's only going to hurt for a little while, but you will get over it. He's not the only man in the world, you know."

Then Finell recalled how after a few more months of emotional turmoil, Mrs. Mimms had pulled her close and rocked her, whispering words of comfort. Then the wise older woman began to quietly reprimand her. "Listen, little girl, you have given that foolish man enough of your grief. Stop looking behind you and press forward. It's obvious that the man is a pea-brained jackass, and I don't believe it was God's plan for you to spend your life married to someone who doesn't appreciate you for the gift you are."

Shaking herself from her reverie, Finell smiled, picked up her cup of tea, toasted her secret friend—"Thank you, my friend"—and took a long, satisfying sip.

Her coworkers watched Finell as she worked through the day with a smile on her face. They thought it was because she was glad to be back at work after being out sick. What they didn't know, and didn't need to know, was that her happiness was coming from her inner thoughts. She kept reviewing Sunday afternoon and evening, and what Joshua had done for her and said to her. The most pleasing memory was that of his soft lips on her cheek.

Still wanting to thank Mr. Hamilton for his kindness, she lifted the phone. Calling his office, she got his answering machine. Disappointed, she managed to make it through the day, and by the time she packed her tote to go home, Finell was in a somber mood. She hadn't seen him all day, and she realized she missed her boss.

She'd always thought of him as a nice-looking man, but the way he'd smiled at her all afternoon on Sunday, she realized just how truly handsome he was. "He's simply beautiful," she said to herself several times throughout the day.

That Monday was an intense day for Joshua. He was stuck in meetings from 8:00 a.m. clear through to 6:47 p.m. with his father, the CEO of the company, and other members of the board. They were meeting to discuss the complaint made against Finell by Devin, the son of one of the board members.

Joshua chose not to have Finell at the meeting. "I'm her superior, and it was my decision to assign her to that position, so I'll accept responsibility for the complaint," he said.

Although he knew he wasn't his father's favorite child or even his choice to succeed him, ever since he was a young man, Joshua had believed if he started from the bottom and worked his way up, his father would change his mind and see him in a different light. So Joshua did just that.

Immediately after college, he had returned to the mail room of U.S. Insurances where he had worked all throughout his high school years. Then he began applying for jobs as they were posted and started his climb up the ladder to his current position.

Edwin Hamilton Sr. didn't dislike his younger son, per se, but he believed Joshua was too compassionate and empathetic to be an effective businessman. He wanted the next head of U.S. Insurances to be a ruthless, cutthroat leader who didn't care what anyone thought about him and plowed ahead and got the job done no matter who got mowed over in the process. He didn't want a man who believed in beginning and ending his days with prayer and treating everyone equally.

However, by the end of the day when the meeting finally concluded, Edwin Sr. realized he was suddenly and reluctantly impressed with his son's executive abilities. Even though he wouldn't admit it out loud, he felt Joshua was becoming quite a good corporate leader—and after the way Joshua handled the executive board meeting, Edwin Sr. had to admit that he liked the way Joshua was running the regional offices to which he had been assigned.

He was impressed with the numbers showing how the region had improved since Joshua had taken over. He was further impressed by the report Joshua made to the board in defense of his appointment of a woman as the regional satellite offices development specialist. Yet as impressed as he was with Joshua, he also believed that all Joshua needed to do was get married. Then he would be able to step up to the next rung on the corporate ladder with no problem.

* * *

Finell's phone rang on Tuesday morning just as she was leaving the house for work. The voice on the other said, "You still sound sexy early in the morning."

David! Finell took a deep breath and rolled her eyes. It seemed no matter what she did, she couldn't get rid of him. For the last few months, he had been trying to make contact with her, but she kept ignoring his calls and text messages.

"David, why are you calling me? What do you want? Why don't you leave me alone?"

"Come on, don't be like that," David said. "Listen, 'Nell, I know you're probably still mad at me, but I want to apologize for how I've been acting. You know we were friends for a long time, and I think we need to be friends again. So, what do you say? Let's go to dinner and talk. I have a lot to tell you."

She couldn't believe him. "David, what we had wasn't a friendship, and I don't want to have anything to do with you anymore."

"What are you talking about? Oh, I know, it's that Hamilton guy, isn't it? Just because he spent Sunday afternoon with you, I'll bet you think he likes you. Well, guess what, girl? That man was just after one thing, and I bet now he's gotten it, you'll probably be left standing all alone and lonesome when he moves on to the next desperate female employee."

"You don't know what you're talking about, David. Please stop trying to contact me. I don't want to have anything to do with you ever again in my life."

He laughed. "You were always so gullible. You gave pretty boy what he wanted, now it should be my turn. I was your man for over three years. We were engaged to be married, and you acted so frigid that I had to turn to someone else to get my love and affection. I should have gotten my chance with you before him, but that's okay. At least I'm going to get it now. It's the least you can do. You owe me!"

Finell was outraged. "You are a fool, David, if you think I'm going to have anything to do with you ever again in my life."

David laughed again. "Okay, 'Nell, I know you don't mean what you're saying. This is me, your first and only real love. Stop trying to be all hard. Now come on, girl, meet me after you get off work before I change my mind."

Finell hung up the phone and left her house. She thought that by the time she'd driven to work, she would have calmed down, but she had to force herself to stay focused all morning to avoid thinking about David and the phone call.

By lunchtime, she was mentally and physically exhausted, so she decided to spend her lunch hour in her office getting caught up on reports. Before she could finish, Joshua knocked on the open door of her office.

"Good afternoon, Miss Everson. I want to talk to you about something. If you can spare the time for me." That stoic expression was back. "Do you have time to talk now?"

"Of course, Mr. Hamilton, please come in."

Following her invitation, Joshua closed the door and sat in the chair at the far corner of her desk. "My father is the CEO of USI," he said, "and he was here yesterday with several other members of the board. They were interested in you."

Before he could say more, Finell stood with her hands resting on her chest, one on top of the other, her face frozen and panicked. "Wh-what? W-why?" she whispered.

Standing and stepping around her desk, Joshua grabbed her shoulders. "Wait, now, don't jump to any conclusions. Just hear me out."

When Finell's shoulders relaxed and she dropped her hands to her sides, Joshua helped her sit back down in her chair. Looking down at her, Joshua felt a strong urge to lift her back to her feet, wrap his arms around her, and kiss her until she begged him to stop. But then he snapped his thoughts back to the reason for his visit to her office.

Sitting back down, Joshua reported, "Devin Martin registered a complaint about us. His father is on the board, and instead of letting Human Resources handle it, they came to me. Martin contended that you aren't as qualified for the satellite offices development specialist position as he is. And he claimed you were awarded the position because I don't like him. But after reviewing your educational background as well as your job performance over the last two years, along with the more than obvious improvements that have been noted in the performance of our satellite offices since your appointment, they all agreed that you were indeed the best-qualified candidate for the job.

"After their information search and data review, the board members concluded that you and I professionally handled everything, and they decided that Devin was trying to use his father's position to force his way into an appointment he didn't deserve."

Finell's eyes flashed with anger, and her mouth formed an O. "I ought to drive down there and punch that contemptible, obnoxious, no-good piece of man in his nose!" she exclaimed.

Laughing, Joshua said, "That's not really necessary, Miss Everson. He's being placed on probation for making a false report and is being sent to the corporate office for retraining." He stood, and once again rounding her desk, he picked up Finell's hands and looked down at her. "I didn't mean to upset you. I just didn't want you to be surprised if you heard anything about yesterday's meetings."

Finell gazed up at Joshua and said, "Thank you."

Lifting her hands slowly, he gently kissed them. "You're more than welcome, Miss Everson."

He offered her a smile and left her office, closing the door quietly behind him. Finell sat staring at her hands before rubbing them on her cheeks.

When he heard the click of the door, Joshua released the air he'd been holding in his lungs. He'd had to hurry and leave her office. He was finding it hard to control himself around her.

"I think I'm falling in love with that woman," he announced to himself, "because I wanted to do more than kiss her hands just then."

For the rest of the day at work, Joshua tried to stay as far away from Finell Everson as possible.

CHAPTER 6

Pacing around his apartment that evening, Joshua felt restless. He just couldn't settle his mind. His thoughts kept focusing on Finell. She'd looked so beautiful to him today in her gray suit with the tangerine blouse and matching shoes.

"As a matter of fact," he mumbled to himself, "she looked downright sexy in that outfit."

Her hair had been in its usual style, brushed straight and held back with a decorative clamp.

"My mistake was to touch her in the first place, but I couldn't help myself. I had to touch her or I was going to lose my mind," he said to the walls of his living room.

"I wonder how her hair looks when it's loose and falling over her shoulders?" He sighed. "I wonder how soft it would feel if I touched it."

Joshua shook his head and smiled to himself. "This woman is driving me crazy. She keeps me off my mark. I think it's time I did something about it."

After work on Wednesday, instead of going directly to church to prepare for prayer service, Joshua made one stop then drove to Finell's house and rang the doorbell.

When she answered the door, he offered her a small bouquet with two roses and some sprigs of baby's breath.

Handing her the bouquet, his handsome face lit up with a smile that made her heart flutter. With that bright, shining smile, Joshua said, "Let me escort you to the company's thirty-fifth-anniversary banquet, Miss Everson."

She accepted the bouquet and returned his smile. "That's five months away," she said, trying to remember how to breathe.

The man was standing close and looking down into her face. She could see now that his eyes were not black but brown, like dark chocolate with sparkling light-brown flecks. His long, thick eyelashes nestled under the heavy, well-shaped eyebrows that completed the picture of sexy bedroom eyes.

Yet his eyes weren't the only things enticing Finell to gaze into his face. His plump, even-colored, smooth, and inviting lips were even more of an attraction. She wanted to feel them gently pressed against hers.

Finell stepped back and invited Joshua into her house. She needed to sit down before her legs collapsed under her. *Oh, my goodness, girl!* she chastised herself. *How could you even go there? This man is just being nice, and here you are thinking he could be interested in you. Stop it!*

When Joshua lightly touched her shoulder and asked, "Do you need time to think about it?" she dragged her mind back to what was happening.

"Aren't you supposed to be somewhere?" she asked him. "Or maybe even be on a date? Besides, like I said, that banquet is five months away. Who knows what things will be like between you and me by then?"

Letting his smile fade, Joshua stepped closer and wrapped his arms gently around her. "Five months gives us time to get to know each other better." Then, sighing, he added, "Miss Everson, I'm going to be honest with you. You have a certain amount of intrigue about you. And it's drawing me in. I want to spend time with you. I want to get to know you as a friend now, and later maybe as more than just a friend. Will you give me that chance?"

Before Finell could answer him, Joshua pressed closer and lifted her chin so that he could look into her eyes.

"I've been praying for months that we could become friends, but what I feel is that we can be more than friends."

He was too close. His body was exuding a quiet strength and power that made her defenseless against his requests. Joshua was holding his breath. He was willing Finell to say yes. When her arms moved to fasten around his waist, he lowered his head slowly, kissed her cheeks, then moved them over, letting his lips press lightly, at first, on hers.

Then, not meaning to deliberately do it, his mouth claimed hers, and he felt her body relax against him. When he realized that he was close to losing control, he broke contact with the plush, sensuous woman in his arms.

After a few tense moments, he stepped back and his smile returned. "What's your answer, woman?" he said, trying to change the atmosphere in the room.

Blushing, Finell said, "Would you give me some time to think about it?"

"Of course. But please don't keep me waiting too long."

They laughed, and Joshua stepped back, not wanting to be away from her tonight. "As to your question, yes, I do have somewhere to be. I should be going to church this evening. Prayer service hasn't started yet." Then he asked, "Would you come with me?"

When Joshua and Finell walked into the small sanctuary together, heads turned and expressions ranged from curious to surprised to bright smiles that said, "Well, it's about time he got himself a woman!"

* * *

The service began with a spirit-filled period of devotion. It opened with the congregation singing "Sanctuary," then after some scripture reading and prayer, the congregation sang "I Give Myself Away." The deacons lead the testimonial period and closed with "Amazing Grace."

Finell was surprised when at the end of the devotional period, Joshua whispered, "Excuse me" and stood to walk to the podium at the front of the sanctuary to present a lesson on hope. He referred the congregation to Jeremiah 17:7: *Blessed is the man that trusteth in the Lord, and whose hope the Lord is.*

He stood behind the podium, opened his Bible, read the scripture, looked at the congregants, and began. "This evening, I have just a few words about hope. Hope is an action word; it means to wait in humble expectation, to trust in something or someone with all your heart. As a believer, having hope is an act of trust in God that He will do all that He has promised us He would do when we put our trust in Him. Having hope is like building a house. Every day, you build that house of hope by reading the Word, believing the Word, trusting the Word, and practicing the Word in the humble expectation that you will be blessed with eternal life. Hope is an investment that doesn't cost you anything, but it gives large dividends in return. If you want to live under the shelter of hope, you should reach out and grip the solid rock.

"Put your hope, your faith, and your trust in Jesus He is the solid rock. He is the rock of our salvation. He is the hope of eternal life. He is, has been, and always will be our earthly representative of the Master, Ruler, and Creator. He is the Son of God, our Father in Heaven, who thought it not robbery to send us His son Jesus to die as a sin offering for you and me. Jesus died but rose on the third day with all power in Heaven and on Earth in His hand, but when He ascended, He did not leave us comfortless He left the Holy Spirit as an assurance that He would never leave us nor forsake us. All we have to do is believe, hope, trust, and obey.

"As the song says, we all should be building our hope on the blood of Jesus and His righteousness. Do you have hope? Are you building a house of hope? Have you been rescued from your sinful actions through confession and baptism? If you are outside the arc of safety tonight, why don't you come on down and let us pray for you? Or, if you are a believer and you feel you need prayer, come down to the altar and let our prayer warriors pray with you."

Joshua raised his hands, and people began to move to the front of the church. For the next forty-five minutes, Joshua and the prayer warriors knelt in prayer with first one person and then another.

Finell had seen Joshua in a new light. Now she understood why he had such a quiet, no-nonsense demeanor about him. "You're a minister," she remarked when he returned to the pew.

"Yes," he said, "I am a minister, but I prefer that you see me as I am: a believer who is trying to live a life that is pleasing to the Lord. It's difficult, but I try to do the best I can."

He took her hands and drew in a deep breath.

"Miss Everson, there's something I want to talk to you about. You and I...we seem to have a connection. What I mean to say is that we seem to be drawn to one another." He looked down at their linked hands and smiled. "Whew! Man, I don't know how to say this. But can we explore this thing that is between us? Can I? May I? Would you allow me to court you?"

NIGHTMARE

As he was talking to Finell, a shadow fell over them and someone said, "Excuse me, sweetheart, but are you going to be much longer? I'm ready to go, and I'm simply starving. We have a date tonight. Remember?"

It was Petra. She was kneeling in the pew in front of Joshua and Finell and smiling.

Then Petra said, "Who is this woman, and why are you holding her hands like that?"

Joshua looked at Petra and then back at Finell. He felt her hands grow tense, and she tried to pull them from his grip. Before releasing her hands, he gripped them, pulled her closer, and kissed her forehead. Then his face regained that no-nonsense expression and he dropped her hands.

Joshua stood slowly and said, "Excuse me, Miss Everson, please?" He looked to the front of the church and beckoned to Pastor Benson, who was just coming out of his office. After speaking briefly with the pastor, he turned to Petra and said, "Follow me, Miss Raymond?"

He left the pew and walked to the front of the church. Petra followed him, an expectant expression on her face.

"What are you trying to do?" Joshua said under his breath. "What kind of game are you playing?"

"What kind of game are *you* playing, Josh, sweetheart?" Petra said. "We are a couple. We were on a date just the other night, and now here you are tonight, out with another woman. How could you do this to me? To us?" Her voice was rising to a level of hysteria, and tears were streaming down her face.

The members of the choir, who had been gathering for practice, all turned to stare at them.

Not caring that they had an audience, Petra launched herself at him. "Josh, you told me you loved me! You said you wanted to be with me."

Joshua put his hands up and grabbed Petra's wrists to keep her from wrapping her arms around his neck. "Petra, why are you doing this? You know you're not telling the truth. I did not say anything like that to you nor did I lead you on at dinner Friday night. The only reason we were out together was because my mother set up the date. I have no interest in you."

She began screaming, "How can you say that to me? Why don't you want me? How can you turn me down? Don't I look sexy to you? You know you want me? I love you, Josh, sweetheart. And I know you love me. Don't do this to us!"

Just then, Deacon Raymond entered the sanctuary and ran to his daughter. "Oh, no. Petra, stop! Don't do this, baby, please, not again!"

"Daddy!" she cried. "Why is he doing this? He told me he loved me. You heard him. He said it when he brought me home. He loves me, I know he does."

"Petra, baby, please don't do this. Not here, baby, please," her father said, his strained voice cracking with sadness. He looked at Pastor Benson and Joshua with pleading eyes. "Please understand. She's been sick. She just got home several weeks ago, and she seemed to be so much better, but I guess she needs more help."

Joshua wrapped an arm around Petra's shoulder. "Listen, Petra, I love you like a child of God. I'm not in love with you because you are not the mate God has chosen for me. Do you understand?"

Sobbing, Petra nodded. "But don't you think I'm pretty? Don't you want me? I can make you feel good. I can make you happy."

With a look of sadness, Joshua said, "You are a child of God who is fearfully and wonderfully made. You have so much to offer someone, but it's not me." Then, looking from Petra to Deacon Raymond and finally to Pastor Benson, he said, "Let's pray."

After the prayer, the deacon walked his weeping daughter out of the church with his arms around, her head on his shoulder. Pastor Benson patted Joshua on the back. "That was good, son."

When Joshua returned to the pew, Finell's eyes were glistening with unshed tears. Instead of saying anything, he offered her his hand and helped her to her feet. Holding hands, they walked out of the church and stood beside his car.

Before helping her into the passenger's seat, Joshua turned Finell to face him and dabbed her eyes and cheeks with his handkerchief. Then he folded her in his arms and gathered her to his chest. "Don't cry," he said. "She's sick, and her father is going to get her some more help."

"That was beautiful. How did you do that? I could not have been that understanding."

Joshua looked down at Finell and smiled sadly. "It's a process that takes much prayer."

As they embraced, Myra Hamilton stood in the shadows watching her son with disapproving eyes. She clicked her tongue and whispered, "Hugging her like that out in public for everyone to see!"

* * *

Pulling into Finell's driveway, Joshua turned to her and said, "Will you think about what I asked you before prayer service?"

She looked across the car at him and smiled. "Well, I've already thought about it."

Joshua shut the engine and walked around the car to help Finell from the passenger seat.

Holding his hand, she said, "Since your invitation was presented in such an eloquent manner, I guess I have no other choice but to say I would be honored, Mr. Hamilton, to have you escort me to the banquet."

Joshua smiled. "And will you come back to prayer service with me next week?"

"Yes," she answered quickly. "I need to learn more about that process of forgiveness. Can you help me?"

"I can try."

For the next six weeks, Joshua and Finell attended Wednesday night prayer service together. And each week after prayer service, they had dinner, just the two of them.

Meanwhile, Myra Hamilton watched her son and the young lady he had yet to introduce to her act as though they were more than friends. She saw how he smiled as they walked together into the sanctuary, his hand resting on the small of Finell's back. Myra observed how close they sat in the pews. She watched as he walked her to his car and hugged and kissed her when they thought no one else was around.

Over time, Myra grew more and more outraged over the situation. She was losing her son to someone who was not worthy of him.

One night after dinner, Joshua and Finell stood at her front door, reluctant to let the evening end. Finally, Joshua took the key from Finell and opened the door. When he handed the key back to her, he held onto her hand and pulled her to him. Easily wrapping his arms around her, he said, "Finell, thank you."

Looking raptly into his eyes, she asked, "For what?"

"For tonight, and for the other times that we've gone out together. For accepting me and what I do without trying to dissuade me from my walk with God, and for making me feel like a man. And especially for letting me court you."

"I respect you, Joshua, and I respect your walk."

"Well, thank you kindly, ma'am," he said teasingly, then slowly lowered his head and kissed her.

This time, it was more than a tentative kiss. This time, it was not a surprise. This time, he kissed her until they were forced to part to catch their breath. Then he leaned in and kissed her breathless again.

Stepping back, Joshua looked at the woman he enjoyed kissing. He loved the way she melted in his arms. This woman that he was drawn to like a moth to a flame, this woman who was soft and curvy, this woman who fit perfectly against his body, made him wonder if it was too soon for him to think about asking for her hand in marriage.

If the truth were to be known, and if he was willing to admit it, Joshua had thought about being married to Finell Everson from the first moment he saw her. He also had to admit that when the engagement between her and David Colwins was voided, Joshua was glad. Not for her heartache, but that he now had a chance to perhaps get close to her. Then he knew that because of his feelings, he needed to pray.

He prayed first and asked forgiveness for coveting another man's love interest. Secondly, he prayed and asked God for the opportunity to get to know Finell better. Then he prayed for her to be his wife.

Now that he had been given the chance to gain her friendship, he wanted to move toward his second most sought-after dream. While his first desire was to be a minister, his second was to be married. As of late, he had been hoping to marry Finell Everson.

Because Joshua and Finell always attended the prayer service together, many of the congregants who also attended began to think of their minister in training and the cute young lady as a couple. For the most part, everyone was happy for them. Everyone, that was, except for Myra Hamilton.

Every Wednesday while Joshua and Finell were having dinner and getting better acquainted, his mother was across town seething with anger. She wanted to know more about the young lady that her son appeared so infatuated with. Even though she didn't know Finell, Myra thought she was a little too worldly for her son.

"All I want is for my son to get married to someone who is on his level, someone who is worthy of his love," she said to her husband. "This woman, for all we know, could be after his money. Do you know that she lets him kiss her in the street? Lord only knows what else she's letting him do to her behind closed doors."

Mr. Hamilton laughed. "Darling, I think you're getting yourself worked up about something that's none of your business."

Myra stared at her husband in disbelief. "Aren't you even concerned about this...supposed relationship? You heard Junior say at dinner a while back that this woman is a model, for heaven's sake! Who knows what type of person she is?"

"Leave the boy alone, Myra. I'm just happy he's showing some interest in a woman. He's thirty years old and doesn't believe in sex before marriage. Maybe this young woman can change his mind."

"Edwin James Hamilton Sr.," Myra said in disbelief, "how could you say such a thing? We don't know that girl, and like I said before, for all we know she's after his money! We don't know anything about her."

Frowning deeply, Edwin Sr. looked intently at his wife. "What is the real problem, Myra? I've never seen you carry on like this before."

"I'm at prayer service every week, and he's never once introduced her to me," Myra said. "Oh, sure. He made a general introduction to the congregation, but he hasn't even thought enough of us to bring her to the house or to Sunday brunch. Why do you

NIGHTMARE

think that is, Edwin? Do we embarrass him? Or is he embarrassed to let us know what type of person she is?"

CHAPTER 7

Most weeks during dinner, Finell and Joshua took the opportunity to discuss any and every subject that came up in conversation. They talked about their childhood. They shared their viewpoints on politics, life in America, and their job responsibilities. They even discussed their past relationships.

One night two months into their courtship, as he was driving her back home, Joshua asked Finell why she would even have considered marrying a man like David Colwins. As they pulled into her driveway, he turned to her and saw she was trying to hold back tears.

Releasing his seatbelt, he jumped out of the car and ran around to the passenger's side, pulled the door open, and helped her out. When she stood, he gathered her in his arms.

"I'm so sorry," Joshua said. "I didn't mean to cause you any pain. I just think you are an amazing woman, and I believe that he's a major loser. I don't see the two of you together, you're too good for him. He is so far beneath you."

In a hushed voice, Finell offered, "Sometimes, Mr. Hamilton, girls like me don't seem to have much of a choice when it comes to having a man in their lives. The majority of men don't like big girls. The majority of men like pretty, petite girly girls who look good on their arms." She looked from his handsome face down at her trembling hands resting on his chest. "And most of the time, if we big girls want companionship, we have to settle for whoever will give us the time of day."

She quieted and pressed her lips together. She didn't want him to see her crying. She didn't want his pity.

Then, her voice wavering, she continued. "I thought David Colwins was my one and only chance to become a wife and mother. But as you well know in the long run, even he didn't want me."

She shrugged her shoulders and tried to step back, but Joshua refused to let her move away from him. "I had no intentions of bringing up hurtful feelings, Miss Everson. It's just that I always thought you could have done so much better than that pitiful excuse of a man." He gave her a crooked smile. "And I think you're wrong about the majority of men. Most men want a woman who has some things in common with him. A man wants someone to share with, someone who is intelligent, honest, and supportive. And if she has those attributes, it doesn't matter to him whether she's a big girl or a small girl."

"Oh, really, Mr. Hamilton?" Finell said playfully.

"Yes, Miss Everson. And I have someone in mind who knows you have all of those attributes and so much more." He smiled down at her with that thousand-kilowatt smile.

"And just who did you have in mind, Mr. Hamilton?"

He looked intently at her, loving that beautiful face, and offered her a hopeful smile. "Me," he said quietly.

Again, she tried to step away from him, but as before, he wouldn't release her. Finell looked up at him in utter shock. *"You?"* she said in surprise.

Joshua nodded slowly. Then, without warning, he lowered his

head and kissed her. Finell grabbed the lapels of his coat and hung on so that she wouldn't fall. That kiss made her want to melt down to the ground like a ball of wax in the hot sun.

He stepped back and took her by her hand. "Let's go inside. We need to talk."

As they walked, he held her hand, and she enjoyed the solace of having him connected to her in such a comforting way. The warmth of his touch seemed to heat her whole body. She felt as though her resolve to not let anyone or anything touch her heart again was beginning to waver.

Once they were seated in her entry hall, Joshua looked into Finell's eyes. "Miss Everson, I've been alone all of my adult life. And now that I'm pursuing my call to ministry, I want to have someone to share my life and make that journey with me. I'm looking for a woman who is compassionate, considerate, and mature enough to make certain decisions by herself. She should be willing to work, making her own money, but still be willing to contribute to the upkeep of the household."

When Finell didn't comment, Joshua took her hands into his and continued. "I've been drawn to you since the day I walked into the USI regional offices and saw you standing by my office door with that bright, honest smile, welcoming me. When I found out that you were involved with someone, I kept hoping that your relationship was not a serious one so that I could have a chance to talk to you. But when you announced your engagement, I thought you were lost to me. Then, when your engagement was called off, I wanted to get close to you, but I didn't want to swoop down on you like a vulture. I knew you needed time to heal, and I wanted to be there to help you. The only way I could think to do that was to become your secret friend."

Finell said nothing, even though she was surprised to find out that he was her secret friend. She wanted to hear everything he had to say. All she had to do was wait for her heart to slow down and stop pounding so loudly in her ears.

"Finell, I'm tired of being alone. And you are the reason for that. Because every time I'm near you, I lose my concentration. When I'm away from you, my mind begins to fill with visions of you. I spend a lot of time wanting to touch you, wanting to kiss you, and wanting to *be* with you. I feel like I'm going to lose my mind if I don't have the chance to make you a permanent part of my life."

Joshua had finally found his opportunity to share his feelings with the object of his affection, and he didn't want to waste the moment. Getting down on one knee before Finell, he continued. "God intends for man and woman to be together in a loving, productive relationship. The scripture tells us that when a man finds a wife, he finds a good thing. And I want to marry you. I want you to be my wife. I want to spend the rest of my life being with you and loving you. I believe you were designed to be my good thing."

"Mr. Hamilton…" Finell said softly, but Joshua tightened his hold on her hands and shook his head, unwilling to let her finish. He was afraid she would tell him that she wasn't interested.

"No, wait, Miss Everson," Joshua said, rubbing his thumbs over the back of her hands and looking deeply into her eyes. "Finell. I want someone to share my journey with me, and I know that you are the one who can do it. Let's get married. What I mean to say is, will you marry me? I think there's something between us that could blossom into a real lasting relationship if we give it a chance."

Finell looked at him with unbelieving eyes. "Me? You want to marry *me*? Where is this coming from?"

Joshua lifted her hands to his mouth and kissed them. "I don't want to lose you. I need to have you in my life," he said as he turned her hands over and kissed her wrists. Then, stopping himself, he added, "You know what? Don't say anything more. Just…just think about this, please."

Gently folding her hands in her lap, Joshua stood, walked across the room, opened the front door, and stepped through it. Then he turned and winked at her and blew her a kiss. "Think about it," he whispered.

* * *

Joshua hadn't been home more than five minutes when an insistent knock began at his door. Looking through the peephole, he asked, "Mom, what are you doing here?"

"Are you going to let me in?" Myra remarked with an edge to her voice. "Or do you have someone here?"

Without saying anything, Joshua stepped back to let his mother into his apartment. "So, how are you, Joshua?" Myra said, her eyes roaming around the apartment.

"I'm fine, Mother, how are you?" Joshua answered as he watched his mother walk from the entry hall into his living room.

"You know, this is such a small place," she said as he followed her. "If you were at home, you would have much more room than this."

"There's just me, Mother, I don't need more room than this."

Myra regarded her youngest son. "Joshua, you are my baby and I want to see you happy before the Lord takes me home. You're intelligent, handsome, and rich. So why don't you have a wife and children? Well, I'll tell you why. Because I haven't found the right woman for you yet, that's why."

"Mom, I don't need—"

Myra held up her hand. "Hush, now. I know what you need better than you do. You don't know your own worth, son. You don't know how to select a woman that will make a good wife for you. You need to have someone in your life who has the social graces and charms that will make you look good to those who can help you make the achievements that will put you at the top of your game."

"Mother…"

Sighing deeply, Myra presented her question to him. "Why haven't we been introduced, son?"

"We who?" he asked, frowning as he walked into the living room to stand beside the couch.

"You know who I'm talking about. That woman that you have allowed yourself to be compromised by. That strumpet you've been bringing to church with you every Wednesday for a while now. I've seen how you look at her, touch her. And yes, I've even seen you *kissing her out in the streets*!" she said with emphasis "That's who!"

Myra grabbed her son's wrists and shook them like he was a four-year-old.

"How could you, Joshy? How could you disrespect your family like that? How could you disrespect the church like that? You are a minister, and you are putting everything you've worked so hard for in jeopardy because of some immoral, overdeveloped…"

Snatching his arms away from his mother's grasp, Joshua said, "Okay, Mother, that's enough!"

He turned his back to her as he walked toward the apartment door. His mother had just tested his patience almost beyond his control. He had no intention of being disrespectful, but he was not about to let her insult the woman he was in love with.

"If you think I'm going to let you stand in my home and be out of line, then you are mistaken," Joshua said. "You need to go."

"What? Are you putting me out of your apartment? She must be here. Is she? Do you have her here? Are you here alone with her?"

Joshua sighed loudly. "Listen, Mother. I don't want to say anything to you that I will later regret, but I'm having a hard time understanding this whole attack on Miss Everson. Is it because she's not one of the women you've been throwing at me over the years? When I was younger and needed you, you had no time to be a mother to me. You let the nanny raise me. Then, when I was too old for a nanny, you stepped in and wanted to take over raising me. Only I didn't need you by then. Now that I'm grown, you want to take over and run my life for me. Well, I don't need anyone to run my life for me. I'm a grown man. I don't need a mother hovering over me waiting to catch me when I fall. There's no more time left for you to raise me in the way I should go. I'm already there, no thanks to you. You're out of time, Mother."

"It's never too late for me to be your adviser and your confidant," Myra said. "I will always be your mother. You have never acted this way before." Her eyes narrowed. "What are you trying to hide?"

Without warning, she ran into the kitchen and looked around. When she found no one there, she turned and ran down the hall to his bedroom. After she had searched his entire apartment including the laundry room, the den, and even the guest bathroom, Myra returned to where Joshua was still standing by the door.

"If you're satisfied, then you may leave now, Mother."

"Son, I'm sorry. But you can't really blame me, can you?" She grabbed his arm. "The least you could have done after all this time was introduce her to your family. You've been acting like you're embarrassed either by us or by her. Which is it, son?"

NIGHTMARE

"Goodbye, Mother," Joshua said as he closed the door in Myra's face. He stood with his left hand resting on his waist and his right arm outstretched, pushing against the door frame, as his head hung down to his chest. "Lord, please forgive me my offenses. It was not my intention to offend anyone, and most of all, to be disrespectful to my mother."

He dropped his hands and walked into his bedroom. This was probably his least favorite place in the entire apartment. It was cold and empty.

Being in this room does nothing more than amplify the loneliness that surrounds me day in and day out, he thought as he lay on the bed with his arms behind his head, staring at the ceiling. Then, aloud, he said, "I believe she is the woman You have chosen for me, and I'm trying to hold on, but I need Your help."

Picking up his nightly prayer book, Joshua turned to the designated lesson and began to read, but he was distracted. His mind kept shifting between his proposal to Finell and his mother's behavior not more than half an hour ago. Finally, he laid the book back on the nightstand, turned off the light, and waited for sleep to come. When sleep had not come by midnight, Joshua picked up his phone and dialed his brother.

"Hey, Josh," Edwin Jr. answered. "What's going on, man, are you alright? This is kind of late for you. What's happening?"

"Yeah, I'm fine," Joshua replied. "I just need to talk. I have a lot on my mind. Can you meet me tomorrow night after I get off of work?"

Edwin Jr. could hear the stress in his brother's voice. "Sure, I can do that. But let me say this to you, man. Whatever it is, don't worry about it. We can work it out. You know us. Brothers by birth, friends by choice. I'm here for you. Now get some rest. We'll talk tomorrow."

* * *

After Joshua presented his proposal and walked out of her house, Finell stood looking at the front door for at least ten minutes. She was in shock. That man had just asked her to marry him.

"Wow!" she exclaimed. "That was a real surprise."

As she prepared for bed, she replayed his words in her head. Sitting on her bed remembering the smile on Josh's face, she heard his final words again as he closed the door: "Think about it."

Finell threw herself back on the bed, kicked her legs wildly above her head, covered her mouth with both hands, and screamed. She rolled onto her side, picked up the telephone, and called her parents.

* * *

Thursday was a long day for Finell. She spent the entire day in her office completing the quarterly reports that were due on Monday. She was having a difficult time keeping her mind on her work. Visions of Joshua holding her hands and looking into her eyes flashed through her mind. She could still feel the sensation of his thumbs rubbing the backs of her hands, could still smell his subtle, woodsy scent, and feel the weight of his lips on hers.

She wanted desperately to go to Joshua's office and ask him if he was serious about his proposal. But the thing she most desperately wanted to do was to walk up to that fine specimen of a man, wrap her arms around his waist, lean her head on her chest, and say, "Yes, yes, yes Joshua. I would love to marry you!"

Of course, she couldn't do anything like that. If she did,

everyone would know they were in a relationship.

"Stop being silly," she whispered to herself. "Why should you care if anyone knows that you and that fine man are in a relationship?" Then, without thinking, she said, "I don't care. I'm just going to go for it!"

"Excuse me, Miss Everson? Did you say you want me to go for your lunch now?"

Snapping her attention back to reality, Finell exclaimed, "Oh, Mrs. Mimms! I was just daydreaming. I'm sorry, let's get back to work."

She settled down and focused on the work before her. She wanted to have everything in order so that she wouldn't have to spend all weekend working. It was time for the scheduled monthly review for the Delta City satellite office, and she was going to be out of the office on Friday.

By the time the reports were finished, it was seven o'clock in the evening and everyone else including Joshua had left the building hours earlier. Mel from building security was standing at her door, ready to escort her to her car, so Finell picked up her tote, her laptop bag, and her purse and followed him to the door.

When she got home, there was a car parked in her driveway that she didn't recognize. As she got out of her car, someone in the other vehicle stepped out from the back seat. It was a woman, but Finell didn't know who she was.

"Excuse me, Miss Everson?" the woman said. "My name is Myra Hamilton. I'm Joshua Hamilton's mother."

Offering her hand, Finell greeted the woman who could someday soon become her mother-in-law. "Good evening, Mrs. Hamilton. It's nice to meet you."

Myra would not take Finell's hand. "Well, we'll see how nice this meeting will be. Please, can we talk?"

Inside the house, Myra stood in the entryway and looked around. "Well, isn't this cozy," she said and smirked. "Listen, *Miss Everson*," she went on, her upper lip curling, "I don't know nor do I care what is going on between you and my son, but I want to let you know that whatever it is, I don't approve. *You* are not the woman that I want my son to be with. *You* have no social standing as far as I can ascertain, and I believe that *you* are a woman of loose morals. Therefore, I suggest you break off whatever is going on between you and my son and walk away."

Finell spun around. "Excuse me?"

"Oh, yes," Myra continued, "I know *about* you. I know that you were engaged to another man two years ago, and I'm quite sure your chosen profession and your lifestyle probably was a great factor in the dissolution of that engagement."

"Mrs. Hamilton, I think that you and I need to get better acquainted before you make assumptions about me."

"Oh, I don't need to know any more about you than I already do, and that's not very much other than the fact you are definitely not marriage material for my son." Then, without further discussion, Myra turned and walked out of Finell's house.

Standing in the open doorway, Finell watched as Myra Hamilton climbed into the back seat of the chauffeur-driven car and was piloted away.

* * *

The following night, Joshua and Edwin Jr. met for dinner after work. "I asked Finell Everson to marry me," Joshua told him.

A broad smile broke across Edwin Jr.'s face. "Well, it's about time," he said. "I thought you were going to be a virgin so long that the top of your head was going to blow off."

NIGHTMARE

"Mom doesn't like Finell." Joshua looked down at his plate, pushed the food around with his fork, and sighed. "Mom showed up at my apartment last night insisting that I was hiding Finell from her. She asked why I hadn't introduced them. Then Mom walked through the apartment looking for her. She feels like Finell has compromised me and is endangering my ministry. Man, Mom was so out of control and disrespectful about Finell that I put her out of my apartment and closed the door in her face."

"Don't worry about that," Edwin Jr. said. "Mom needs to be shut down every once in a while. She's been trying to control my life for years. Why do you think I became a pilot and started my own business rather than go into the family business? So I could get away from Dad and her, that's why." Shifting the focus of the conversation, Edwin Jr. leaned forward and looked into his younger brother's eyes. "Do you love her?"

Without hesitation, Joshua said, "Yes. I love her and I want her in my life."

"Do you love her like a friend, like your mother, or like a woman you want to spend the rest of your life with?"

"I want her by my side for the rest of my life. I feel fulfilled when I'm with her."

Edwin Jr. reached out and clapped his brother on his back. "Man, you've got it bad. And if that's the case, then, you better marry her before someone else gets to her."

Joshua laughed. "Yeah? Someone like who?"

Edwin Jr. grinned teasingly. "Someone like me. Who do you think? You know I'm the handsome one, and I've got the most magnetic personality. I've never met a woman who could resist me. Don't let me walk up and throw my mack down on her, 'cause you know for sure she'll be mine in a nanosecond."

Joshua laughed. "Don't think more highly of yourself than you should, big brother. The fall from grace is a long fall into a bottomless pit."

* * *

Later that night, a little more than twenty-four hours after her phone call to them, Finell's parents knocked on her front door.

"Mom? Dad?" she said, surprised. "What are you doing here? How did you get here so fast?"

General Alphonso Everson said, "Don't worry about that, just let us in, please." As they stepped into their daughter's house, her father continued, "You know that we love you, and the last time you were engaged, I knew you were with a fool. We need to meet this one face to face, just to make sure that your judgment has improved. You know I need to have a son-in-law that I like!"

"Well," Finell said, "you're going to love Joshua Hamilton. He's an amazing man. He's loving and kind." She dropped her arms from her parents' shoulders and looked down at the floor, trying to control her emotions, then took a deep breath. "And…and…oh, Mom, Dad, what am I going to do? His mother hates me. She thinks I'm leading her son astray."

When her tears fell, her mother held her. "Calm down now, Finell. What makes you think the woman hates you?"

Leading her parents through the house into the kitchen, Finell put water in the tea kettle and began preparing lunch as she told her parents what happened between her and Myra Hamilton. Listening intently to their daughter, Alphonso and Karina Everson resolved to meet with the parents of their daughter's new fiancé.

Karina thought to herself, *I'm going to make it my mission to get in that woman's face.* Meanwhile, Alphonso determinedly thought, *I'm going to speak to that young man's father. He needs to get his wife in order.*

NIGHTMARE

When Finell finished recounting the details of the situation, she was asked by her father to "Tell me about Joshua."

Her parents noticed the swift change in their daughter's body language. She sat straighter in the chair. She smiled so brilliantly that her face began to glow. And her voice became musical. With her eyes fixed on a spot on the wall across the room, she sighed and began. "Joshua Hamilton is the most fascinating man I've ever met. He has a brilliant mind. He's emotionally stable and always in control. His posture is straight just like yours, Dad. He doesn't smile much, but when he does, he lights up a room."

Finell smiled through the tears in her eyes.

"He has a soft heart. When he holds me, I feel cocooned and protected. I've always been treated like a lady by him, and he wants nothing from me other than my love and devotion. He speaks softly, has a gentle touch, doesn't care that I'm a big girl, and he's a minister in training at his church."

"Oh, baby," Karina said, hugging her daughter. "We can't wait to meet your young man."

Trying to lighten the moment, her father said, "Well, I can certainly wait. I'm tired. Let's eat so we can go to bed."

CHAPTER 8

It had been two days since Joshua and Finell had seen each other. On Thursday, he was still angry with his mother and was in no mood to talk to anyone other than his brother. He was afraid to talk to Finell because he didn't want to hear her turn down his proposal. But that only lasted until Friday. That morning, Joshua called Finell as she was on her way to Delta City.

When her phone rang, Finell pushed the connector button on her steering wheel and said, "Hello?"

"Hello yourself," Joshua said. "How are you this morning?"

"Well, it's been almost two whole days since I've seen or talked to you. I guess I'm doing as well as can be expected. How are you this morning and what can I do for you, Mr. Hamilton?"

"You can let me see your beautiful face tonight so I can taste those delicious lips, drown in those deep liquid eyes, and hold your warm and tender body in my arms," Joshua said.

Finell blinked to clear her misty eyes. She couldn't respond to what she'd just heard.

"Finell," Joshua said, "are you there?"

Clearing her throat, Finell said, "I don't know how to respond to what you just said. No one has ever said anything as beautiful as that to me."

"Well, get used to it, Miss Everson. Because I'm courting you, and I intend to say things like that to you for the rest of my life. That is, if you agree to become my wife."

Finell beamed. "Well, I've never been courted before, and if this is what courting is about, then yes, I am honored to become your wife."

With a low, husky tone to his voice, Joshua said, "I love you, Finell Everson."

"I love you, Joshua Hamilton," she replied in a soft, sweet voice.

His voice sounded strained when he asked, "Can we spend the evening together?"

"My parents are visiting and they want to meet you," Finell said. "By all means, come by this evening. I'll be home as close to 5:15 as I can."

* * *

Joshua spoke to himself as he drove to Finell's house that evening to meet her parents. "Okay, mister. You better make a good first impression. You know that the first one is a lasting one."

The woman who opened the door was an older but just as amazingly beautiful version of Finell. "Well, now, you must be Joshua Hamilton," she said in a pleasant musical tone. "Please, come in." Then, offering her hand, she said, "I'm Karina Everson, Finell's mother."

When he stepped through the door, Joshua found himself looking at a man with a stern face and ramrod-straight posture. With a firm handshake, the older gentleman said, "Good evening, young man, I'm Alphonso Everson. It's nice to meet you. Now, come on in so we can get better acquainted."

Four hours later as he was leaving Finell's house, Joshua realized the Eversons were good people who loved their daughter and wanted only the best for her. He also realized he was going to have to calm down a lot before he arrived at his parents' house, but that didn't happen. As soon as he used his key to let himself in and called out to them, he knew that what was about to happen could go very badly. Especially if he didn't practice some self-control and remember that his parents loved him, even though sometimes their actions didn't show it.

Edwin Sr. stepped out of the family room, followed by Edwin Jr. "Hello, son," his father said. "I have a sneaking suspicion that you want to talk to us."

Mr. Hamilton walked to the staircase and called to his wife. As she was descending the stairs, she said, "Edwin, dear, you mustn't yell. We *do* have an intercom, you know."

When Myra looked at Joshua, she almost missed the last step. His face looked very angry. But rather than confront him, she decided to placate him. "Hello, Joshy, what brings you by tonight?" She raised her arms to hug her son, but he quickly stepped away from her.

"Don't touch me. I'm very angry with you," Joshua said as he put one hand on his hip and smoothed his hair with the other hand. "I just left Finell's house. Her parents are visiting, and we talked. Finell told us about the conversation you had with her Thursday night. She told me everything you said and did. You invaded her privacy with your background check, you told her she wasn't good enough to be my wife. How could you? Why did you do that?"

"Son, I was doing my duty as your mother. I was protecting you."

Frustrated, Joshua turned to his father and his brother. "Finell and I have been going out for almost three months, and on Wednesday evening, I asked her to marry me." Then he turned back to his mother. "That was just before you came by and searched my apartment thinking she was there. But that wasn't enough for you was it, Mom?" He sneered, the volume of his voice escalating. "You had to go to her house and tell her she's not the right woman for me. You told her she wasn't good enough to be my wife."

"What?!" Edwin Sr. yelled.

Beside him, Edwin Jr. whispered, "Oh, damn!" under his breath.

Myra stepped closer to Joshua but didn't dare touch him. "Joshy, son, you may be angry now, but you're going to thank me later when you realize she's not good enough for you. She's probably only after your money. Why, she's a model, for goodness' sake! What kind of wife would a woman like that make? You should be glad I'm concerned about you and your future. After all, the wrong relationship can ruin your life."

"What wrong relationship?" Joshua snapped. "The only wrong relationship I have right now is being your son!"

Edwin Sr. stepped forward and touched his son's shoulder. "Be careful, Josh. Don't let your anger make you cross the line."

Joshua looked at his father and nodded his head. Then, to his mother, he said, "You don't even know Finell. She's a beautiful, intelligent, and hardworking young lady."

"Joshy, she takes her clothes off in front of cameras! You deserve better than that!"

Seeing that his brother was becoming increasingly frustrated and that his level of anger was rising, Edwin Jr. put his hand on Joshua's shoulder. "Mom, Finell Everson has been a model since she was in college, and she is one of the most preferred plus-sized catalog models in the country."

"What about her family?" Myra said. "What kind of people are they? And how could they let their daughter get into a profession like that?"

She was determined to sway her son from the clutches of Finell Everson. After Joshua first brought her to the Wednesday night services, Myra had a background check run on Finell. Even though the report showed nothing out of the ordinary, she thought that if she pressed the issue of modeling being an unethical profession, her son would lose interest in the girl.

She knew Joshua was not one to go against her wishes. He had always been obedient and respectful, but now he was standing in front of her with his eyes full of anger and his face filled with rage. Myra was convinced that Finell was the reason for his rebellion.

Joshua regarded his mother. She'd been known to pull many a harebrained stunt in her time, and for the most part, they had been harmless. But this time, he felt she'd gone too far.

"Mom, I'm sure you know from that background report you did on her that Finell's father is a retired two-star general. Her brother is a professor of international economics at Harvard and is on the budgetary advisory board for the president of the United States. Her sister is a chemist who works in the family business. Mrs. Everson is the only child and heir to the Waterstone family corporation, which creates and manufactures its own line of hair care, skincare, and makeup products for people of color. They are a good, stable family."

Mr. Hamilton looked at his wife. "So you went and pried into the girl's background? Are you crazy? Myra, I told you to leave the boy alone. I told you to stay out of his business!"

"Well, excuse me!" Myra growled. "I was only doing my duty as a mother. How was I supposed to know any of this stuff? He never introduced us to that girl. I had to know what kind of person she is. We can't let just anybody into this family. We operate within a strict social profile, and we have societal obligations to maintain."

Edwin Sr. spoke through thinned lips. "Really, Myra? After all of this, you're wondering why the boy didn't want you to have any contact with her?" He shook his head and turned to face his youngest son. "Josh, try to calm down, son. She didn't turn you down, did she? What can we do to fix this?"

"No, she didn't turn me down. She loves me, and for some unknown reason, she believes that she and Mom can become friends. I told her not to count on it."

Always the helpful older brother, Edwin Jr. asked, "So, what are your plans?"

"We're getting married in two months," Joshua said with a bright smile.

"Two months?" Myra gasped. "That's not enough time to plan a proper wedding. I'm going to have to pull in a lot of favors for this."

Pointing at his mother, Joshua spoke in a voice he was trying hard to control. "You are not going to have anything to do with the planning of this wedding. I want you to stay as far away from Finell and her family as humanly possible until the day of the wedding. And then all you're going to do is sit with Dad and keep your mouth closed! That is, if we even let you attend the wedding."

Myra folded her arms over her chest. "Is she pregnant? Have you let her compromise your position in the church? Is that why you want to get married so fast?"

Joshua looked at his mother with deep hurt in his eyes before he walked through the front door of his parents' house.

When he was gone, Edwin Jr. emitted a mirthless chuckle. "Mother, this little stunt may have cost you dearly. Josh has never had a physical relationship with a woman. He loves her, and I'm sure they are both committed to waiting until they're married to have sex."

Myra looked at her son and then her husband. "Well, you can't be too careful these days. I only have his best interests at heart."

Edwin Sr. shook his head. "I'm only saying this one last time, Myra. Leave the boy alone or you'll lose him."

* * *

Joshua nervously paced the lobby of the church. He was waiting for Finell and her parents to arrive. He'd sent the church van to her house. The plan was to have them all attend church services, then drive to the Hamilton Hotel for lunch.

When they arrived, he escorted them into the sanctuary. Once inside, Joshua looked at his mother but didn't stop to introduce her to the Eversons before, during, or even after service. Myra Hamilton was put out with her son for having guests in church without following proper protocol.

Later that afternoon, Joshua held Finell's hand as he led the group into the restaurant. When they stopped at the table where his family was seated, Joshua slid his arm around Finell's waist and said, "Mom, Dad, I want to introduce you to my fiancée. Her name is Finell Everson, and these are her parents, General and Mrs. Everson."

Still feeling the sting of her son's snub from church, Myra tried to protest but Edwin Sr. stood up and offered his hand. "General. Mrs. Everson. It's a pleasure to meet you. Please have a seat. We would be honored to have lunch with you." Then he turned to Finell. "And you, young lady, it is a great pleasure to finally make your acquaintance."

NIGHTMARE

Smiling, Finell thanked the charming gentleman. Before she could sit, she was lifted from the floor by someone who had come up behind her, folded their arms around her waist, and picked her up. "So, you're going to settle for second best when you can have the cream of the crop! What is wrong with you, woman?"

When he set her back on her feet, she turned to face him. "EJ?" she said, her smile broadening as she embraced him. "Hello! What are you doing here?"

"Finell Everson," Joshua said, shaking his head and grinning, "the gentleman that you call EJ is my brother, Edwin Hamilton Jr."

While all of the introductions were going on, Myra said not one word. She couldn't believe her son would bring these outsiders into their Sunday family time.

As the meal progressed, the conservation flowed easily around the table between everyone. Everyone, that was, except for one person. Myra smiled tightly and only spoke when she was addressed directly. And it was noticeable that Joshua did not look at or even speak to his mother.

Myra was not a happy person. She did not in any way approve of the relationship between her son and Finell. She knew Joshua had great potential, and it was her belief that with the right woman as his wife, he could be a very successful businessman. She was also certain that Finell "the plus-size model" Everson was *not* the right woman for her son.

I've got to do something about this mess! she thought to herself. But in the meantime, she had to put an end to this family bonding-time fiasco.

After quietly taking out her phone and sending a text message, Myra picked up her goblet and poured some of the water onto her napkin. Then, pressing it to her forehead, she quietly moaned,

"Oh, I'm so very sorry, everyone, but I seem to be getting one of my sick headaches." She looked at her husband and said just above a whisper, "Dear, I'm going to have to get home and go to bed."

Mrs. Everson reached out and touched Myra's shoulder. "I'm so sorry for you, dear. You should by all means get home and rest." With that said, General Everson was immediately behind Maya's chair, helping her to stand.

Not looking very pleased with the situation, the senior Mr. Hamilton took his wife's arm. "Alright, everyone, let's not get too excited. Please, take your seats. Don't let this unfortunate situation chase you away. We are going home, but we want you all to stay and enjoy your meal."

Before his parents could walk away, Joshua stood. "Dad, would you wait for just a moment, please?"

When everyone stopped doting on his mother, Joshua turned and looked around the table. Then he looked down at Finell, took her hand, and lifted her from her chair.

"I wanted to do this in front of the people that mean the most to us," Joshua said. "So since everyone is here now…" He lowered himself to one knee. "Finell Everson, I fell in love with you the first time I saw you, and I want to spend the rest of my life being with you, loving you as my wife and prayerfully the mother of our children."

Finell looked at him and her heart soared. Joshua's voice had such a captivating and mesmerizingly rich tone that it felt like she was being hypnotized. She was so enraptured with the man kneeling before her that she knew she would follow him anywhere without question or reservation.

Joshua's hand tightened on her wrist. "Finell. Baby. Will you marry me?" Finell lifted her other hand to her mouth, trying not to let the sobs escape.

"Oh, that is so beautiful!" Karina Everson gushed when Joshua slipped the 2-carat diamond cluster solitaire wide-band platinum engagement ring on Finell's finger.

Edwin Jr. stood behind Joshua, looking at the ring with his mouth open. "Wow, brother. That's a real nice piece of jewelry."

Realizing that Finell had not yet consented to the proposal, the General and Mr. Hamilton both spoke at the same time. "Well, don't keep the man waiting. Answer him."

Looking from the ring to the man kneeling before her, Finell reached out and tenderly touched his handsome face. "Joshua Hamilton, I would be honored to spend the rest of my life with you as my husband and the father of our children. Yes. Yes, I will marry you."

Joshua stood, gathered Finell in his arms, folded her against his chest, and whispered, "Thank you" in her ear as his lips caressed her neck. Then he raised his head, leaned forward, and kissed her. Softly. Gently. Unhurriedly.

Just then, Myra fell into her husband's arms with a gasp as she watched her son do something she was sure would ruin his life. She turned her back to the couple, refusing to accept the situation. Joshua reached into the inside pocket of his jacket, pulled out his handkerchief, and blotted the tears from his fiancée's cheeks, paying no attention to his mother at all.

Frustrated that her son was still going against her wishes, Myra stormed from the restaurant, ranting, "This is not something that I'm going to accept! It's a good thing I thought ahead. I have a plan, and it will work, and I will get my way. This girl had better enjoy herself now because Joshua is not going to be with her too much longer. Ring or no ring, my Joshy will *not* get married to Finell Everson!"

* * *

"Little brother, you are the man!" Edwin Jr. said an hour and a half later as the remaining members of the party were leaving the restaurant. "That ring is impressive. I didn't know you had it in you."

As they stepped onto the restaurant parking lot, they heard a woman cry out in surprise. She ran toward Joshua with her arms outstretched, gushing, "Oh, Josh! It is you, isn't it? It's so good to see you! It's been a while, how have you been?"

It was obvious to Finell that Joshua was not pleased to see the screaming woman as he quickly stepped back and away from her, avoiding her and her outstretched arms. Without a word, he looked her up and down with steely eyes. He tightened his hold on Finell's hand and smoothly stepped away from the group, pulling his new fiancée toward his car.

Walking quickly to keep up with her hand still in his, Finell asked, "Joshua, who is she? And why are being so rude to her? I've never seen you act this way."

"Let's just go," he said and opened the passenger door. "Get in! Please."

He looked upset. Rattled. Finell had never seen him so unsettled. Rather than cause a scene, she slid into the passenger seat and allowed him to close the door. There was no conversation as the newly engaged couple traveled to Finell's house. When he pulled into her driveway, Joshua turned to Finell. "I'm sorry about my behavior at the restaurant," he said, "but I was surprised to see that woman."

"Who is she?"

"Her name is Marlee Turner. We went to school together from junior high through our junior year of college. Her parents and mine were best friends until there was an argument. And one day, she and her family moved out of town without warning, under cover of darkness. I never heard from or saw her again until today, just now."

"But why are you so upset?"

"It doesn't matter," he said and kissed her. "I'm not upset. I was just surprised."

They sat in the car for a few minutes, looking at each other, Joshua thinking, *I've got to tell her. But only when I get past the anger.*

Finell thought Marlee Turner must have been an old girlfriend of Joshua's. Maybe the one who broke his heart. Not waiting for Joshua to be the gentleman that he was, she opened the car door and stepped out. "Good night," she said. "I'll see you in the morning."

Joshua stepped out of the car and leaned over the top. "Don't forget that we're going to tell our coworkers tomorrow," he said as Finell walked into her house and closed the door.

At that moment, Edwin Jr. pulled into the driveway behind Joshua and got out. "Man, you left them at the restaurant!" he said. "This is not a good way to treat your potential in-laws, little brother."

Alphonso Everson helped his wife out of the car, and as they were walking toward the front door, he said to Joshua, "Get it straight before you marry her, son. Good night."

* * *

Monday morning found Joshua and Finell feeling tired and worn. Neither had gotten a full night's sleep. Joshua was trying to think how he was going to tell Finell the story about Marlee Turner. Finell was afraid that the return of the old girlfriend was going to put an end to the engagement.

Looking into the mirror trying to conceal the dark smudges under her eyes, Finell shrugged her shoulders. "Oh, well. It won't be my first broken engagement because of another woman. I will survive."

As she pulled into her parking stall at work, Finell heard someone calling out to her. "Excuse me. Excuse me. Miss? Hello?"

Turning around, Finell saw the woman from the restaurant.

"May I speak with you please?" Marlee said. "I promise I won't keep you long."

Finell didn't answer.

"In case you don't already know, my name is Marlee Turner. I'm in love with Joshua Hamilton. We have a child together. His name is Joseph Turner Hamilton. He's never met Joshua, and now that he's older, he wants to meet the man who is his father. That's why I'm here. But believe me, I don't want to cause any problems."

The smile on Marlee's face was so insincere that Finell almost laughed. She looked at the petite, well-dressed woman before her. She was simply beautiful, and she made Finell feel like an ugly stepsister standing in front of her dressed in her high-end outfit.

"I'm just here to let you know that I made a mistake by leaving all those years ago," Marlee said. "Now I'm here to get my man back."

Without a word, Finell went into the building and took the elevator to her office, closed the door, and waited for the staff meeting to begin.

* * *

Finell sat through the meeting, noticeably distracted. Joshua thought it was because of the announcement he was going to make at the end of the meeting.

When it was time, he cleared his throat and said, "Miss Everson, will you come join me here, please?" With Finell at his side, he lifted her hand. "Over the weekend, Miss Everson and I became engaged. We plan to be married in a small, private ceremony. But we will have a reception, and you are all invited."

After the initial surprise faded, everyone congratulated the couple and wished them lasting happiness. When everyone had left the conference room, Joshua closed the door and lowered the blinds.

"So," Joshua said, "do you want to tell me what's wrong?" He stood in a wide-legged stance with his hands clasped behind his back.

"No," was all Finell said before she snatched the door open. She managed to make it to her office without having to stop, but when she saw a picture lying on top of her desk, she felt her chest tighten in anger and fear. She picked it up to see the smiling faces of Marlee Turner and a little boy who looked to be about ten or eleven years old.

Taking a deep breath and squaring her shoulders, Finell spun around and slammed into Joshua's rock-hard chest. His hands quickly rose to her elbows, but she pushed herself away from him. Releasing her arms, Joshua stood looking at her intently.

"Fin? What's wrong?" he asked, his voice tight.

She returned his gaze for a few moments before she spoke. Finally, she said, "This morning, the woman from the restaurant last night was waiting for me when I arrived at work. She told me that you and she have a son together. She said that your son wants to finally meet you. His name is Joseph Turner Hamilton. She also told me that she's in love with you and intends to get her man back."

Looking at the picture, Finell continued, "She's apparently been in my office, because here's a picture of her and your son. I'm sure she meant for you to have this picture. And oh, yes, while I'm at it, here's your ring back. Have it resized and give it to her, if you like. Since I didn't pay for this one, I won't be keeping it!"

She slammed the picture into his chest, but before she could take the ring off, Joshua grabbed her hands and held them. "Wait, Finell," he said as she tried to get away. "Stop, please." He shook her lightly. "Let me tell you something I should have told you last night."

"Now?" she exclaimed. "Now you want to tell me something?" She looked into his beautiful, pleading eyes. Instead of snatching away from him, she sighed and skeptically relented. "Okay, what?"

"Not here. Come with me. Get your purse and your keys," he told her." When she hesitated, he added, "If you love me, you have to trust me."

He dropped her hands and left the office. By the time she'd retrieved her purse from her desk drawer and caught up with him, Joshua was standing at the secretary's desk, telling her that they would be out of the office until after lunch.

"Alright, now," Mrs. Mimms said, smiling widely and winking. "You two better behave yourselves."

They got into Joshua's car, and as he drove, he called his brother. "EJ," he said, "I need you to bring me that envelope I asked you to store for me. Meet me at USI's corporate park."

Several minutes later, they arrived at a park filled with colorful flower beds and lots of trees. After a short walk across the brick path from the parking area to the designated dining area, Joshua and Finell arrived at a small gazebo.

Edwin Jr. was waiting for them. He hugged them both, but to his brother, he asked, "What happened?" After hearing the short explanation, EJ shook his head and handed Joshua an envelope.

"So, do you think this is some of Mom's handiwork?"

"I don't want to think that it is," Joshua said, "but I have to say yes. I believe this is some of her mess."

Shaking his head, EJ hugged his brother again and kissed Finell's cheek before leaving them alone. Joshua opened the envelope and pulled out a DNA report.

"What I told you last night was true," Joshua told Finell. "I did go to school with Marlee, and our parents did have a fight that ended their friendship. The fight happened when I was nineteen and I was accused of being the father of Marlee's unborn child. Marlee tried to bribe me with money from her trust fund to say I was the father. I refused, of course, and her father tried to force me to marry her. The situation turned uglier when I was accused of rape and suspended from the university. Her parents had me placed on house arrest. But when the DNA results were inconclusive, her parents were embarrassed and left town right after. I have not seen nor heard from her until now."

When she didn't respond, Joshua moved closer to Finell. "Listen, I'm sorry. I was wrong. I should have told you about this. But I honestly never thought I would see Marlee ever again. So, to me, there was no reason to dredge up the past."

"But she's still claiming that her son is your child," Finell said, reading the report. "The little boy does look a little like you, and this report says there's a familial strain to the DNA in the results. So is the father one of your relatives?"

"It's my cousin Irvin Jr.'s baby," Joshua said sadly. "His father is my father's twin brother. Marlee and my cousin were secretly going together when we were in our sophomore and junior years of college. I never said anything because I didn't want to ruin his marriage. When she accused me of being the cause of her pregnancy, I kept expecting Irv to do the right thing and admit what he had done. Because he didn't, we no longer associate with one another."

Slowly reaching for Joshua's hand, Finell asked, "So now what are we going to do about this woman and her lies?"

Joshua was surprised. "You're not angry?"

"Please know that I am very angry," she said, "but not with you. That woman lied to my face while demeaning my fiancé. And for some unknown reason, she thinks I'm going to just lay down and let her believe she can take my man from me? Oh, no. She picked the wrong one at the wrong time. She's going to find out just who she's messing with."

Joshua took Finell's hand. "Hold on just a little bit, baby. Let me handle it. The first thing I'm going to do is get my mother and Marlee together. Then I'm going to confront them with their lies."

CHAPTER 9

"**H**ow did it go this morning?" Myra asked Marlee.

"She was surprised, but she didn't say anything," Marlee reported. "She was looking at me like she wanted to slap my face, then she turned her back to me and walked into the building before I could give her the envelope. However, I did get the chance to put the picture on her desk while they were in a staff meeting." Then, as if needing reassurance, she added, "Miss Myra, do you think this is really going to work? Joshua didn't seem happy at all to see me."

"Don't fret, Marlee. You know my Joshy has never been able to deny someone in need. When he hears the story we're going to tell him, he'll drop her and focus on you and your little one. Besides, I'm his mother, and when he knows I'm serious about him not being with her, he'll do everything he can to make me happy. Don't worry, he'll come around. He always does."

* * *

After he and Finell returned to the office, Joshua called Edwin Jr. for a favor.

"Can you please call Mom and ask her to come by my apartment this evening? Tell her that Finell is trying to break off the engagement. I'm sure she'll show up then."

At seven o'clock, the doorbell to Joshua's apartment rang. When he opened the door, he wasn't surprised by what he saw: his mother and Marlee Turner, standing side by side and smiling like they'd just won the lottery.

Rushing forward, Marlee threw her arms around his neck. "Oh, Josh. Miss Myra told me that you called off your engagement. And that you wanted to see me. Thank you. I knew you would come to our rescue, Josh. I love you so much. I'm going to be so good to you, you'll see. I'm going to make sure you don't remember anything about her at all."

Pulling her arms from his neck, Joshua stepped aside and invited the two women into his apartment.

Myra's first words were, "My goodness, something smells delicious, son. What are you cooking?"

"I thought we could all have some dinner after we talk…if you feel like it by then. You don't mind, do you, ladies?"

The women looked at each other and smiled. "You're still so nice and sweet," Marlee said. "Having dinner with you sounds very nice. We don't mind at all."

He ushered the two into the living room and offered them a seat. Not wanting to waste time, Joshua began, "There's a lot that I want to know, so I'm going to get right to the point of this meeting. To begin with, let me ask you—what kind of game are you playing, Marlee? Why are you back in town? How dare you tell my fiancée that your child is my son? How could you lie like that?"

Myra held up her hand. "Wait, now, Joshy, let me say something first. You know that your dad and I are Marlee's godparents, and over the years since her family took her away, she and I have kept in contact with one another."

Without waiting for a response, she pressed forward with her plan to garner her son's sympathy for the girl she wanted him to marry.

"I've been there for her and little Joey from the beginning. Marlee's mother and father stopped supporting her right after little Joey turned ten. And they have managed to regain control of her trust fund, also. The girl needed someone to help her. Son, I know that you are the right person to continue to give her what she and Joey so desperately need. Because she has no job, they have no money and no place to stay right now, other than in our guest cottage. They need you."

A long silence stretched across the apartment. Marlee stood and walked across the room to stand beside Joshua. She raised her hand and caressed his back. He looked at her, and the intensity of that look made her drop her hand and take a step away from him.

"What makes you think that I want to have anything to do with you after what you did to me?"

"Josh," Myra said, "that was almost twelve years ago."

"I was a scared young girl back then," Marlee said. "Besides, it wasn't my idea to say that you were the baby's father." She reached up to touch his shoulder but dropped her hand. "I was hoping that by now you would know how sorry I am and forgive me. I was young, scared, and alone, Josh. I needed you."

Ignoring the excuses, he continued his directives to Marlee. "You lied and tried to manipulate me into becoming part of your duplicitous behaviors. I've been praying for you over the years, and I have forgiven you. But there is no way that I will let you back into my life!"

Marlee knew the conversation was not going the way she and Joshua's mother had anticipated. She stepped closer and looked into his eyes. "Do you remember when we were in school together and how, during our study times, we promised each other that we would get married someday? You made a promise to me, and I want you to know that I'm holding you to your promise."

"I'm not a fourteen-year-old with stars in his eyes anymore, Marlee. I'm a grown man with real adult feelings and emotions. I won't let you and my mother manipulate me into a situation that is not right for me or you, and especially not right for your son."

Marlee wasn't listening to his words. She was still trying to engineer a comfortable life for herself and her son. "You should have been there to protect me, Josh, and keep me on the right path when we went to college. If you had done that, we would be married, and you, Joey, and I would be a happy family right now."

Joshua picked up the picture that Marlee had put on Finell's desk. "We can't be a family Marlee. I don't love you."

"Stop being silly, son," Myra countered. "Love is not that important at the beginning of a marriage. You can grow to love her. She already loves you, and Joey looks enough like you that people would come to believe that he's yours. The boy is eleven years old and has never had a father in his life. How can you let this child suffer needlessly?"

Still looking at the picture, Joshua said, "Tell us who your son's father is, Marlee."

Marlee's eyes grew wide. "No, Josh, no. Don't do this!"

Without blinking, he said, "Answer the question, Marlee. Who is the father?"

Tears began to roll down Marlee's face. "Why are you doing this? I thought you loved me. You know that I love you. We can be happy together, Josh. I know we can be good together. I'm sure you will be a wonderful father to Joey."

"Marlee, tell the truth. Who is your son's father?"

NIGHTMARE

"You know it's your cousin Irvin Jr.'s son!" she wailed. "I was a gullible young girl back then. My being with your cousin was your fault. If you had been my boyfriend like I wanted, then your cousin wouldn't have enticed me into a relationship with him." Marlee turned to Myra and lifted her hands. "Miss Myra, Irvin, Jr. used to come to the campus every Friday night, and we would spend the whole weekend together. When I told him I was pregnant, he accused me of being whorish and said I should have been smart enough not to let that happen. He refused to even acknowledge the baby because he was married by that time. So now that he and his wife haven't had any children, he wants to claim his son and take full custody."

Turning back to face Joshua, Marlee threw her arms around him. "Josh, you've got to help me. Your mother said that she could get you to marry me and solve all my problems. Please, Josh, I need you. Joey and I, we both need you. Help us. Don't let us down."

Pulling her arms from his waist, Joshua moved away from Marlee and walked out of his living room into the kitchen. Myra and Marlee heard him speaking to someone. "Have you heard enough? I certainly hope so, because I don't think I can be any more disgusted with them and this whole situation than I am right now."

When he returned to the living room, Joshua was holding Finell's hand. They were followed by Edwin Sr. and his twin brother, Irvin Sr.

"So it's true, isn't it, Miss Turner?" Irvin Sr. said. "Little Joseph is my grandson? All you had to do was come to us. My wife and I would never have turned you away. There was and is no reason for Joseph to be subjected to what you're putting him through when his family can provide all his needs and most of his wants." Turning to his sister-in-law, he added, "Thanks for all you've done over the years, Myra, but we will be taking over from here."

Marlee covered her face with her hands and began sobbing. Myra stepped beside her and put her arm around her shoulder. Then she looked at Finell and said through gritted teeth, "Why don't you just go away? None of this had to happen. How could you have the nerve to stand between her and the happy life she should be having with my son? She would make a much better wife for him than you could. After all, she has been trained in the social graces that a young wife would need to make her husband successful."

Finell stepped forward but was halted when Joshua wouldn't release her hand. As his other arm moved around her waist, anchoring her to his side, she said, "Because I love this man, I'm going to try not to be too disrespectful to you, Mrs. Hamilton. But are you out of your mind? It is beyond my comprehension that Joshua could have grown into the amazing man he is today with a mother like you. Have you ever loved him?"

"How dare you speak to me like that!" Myra exclaimed. "My Joshy is special and deserves only the best. His happiness is my happiness. There is no place for you in our lives. You are trying to take him away from me. And I won't have it!"

"How can you love him and not want him to be who he is? Love is constant, not selective. Love is encouraging and uplifting. Not demeaning and selfish." Finell's voice had risen above her usual level and was becoming shrill. Joshua could feel her trembling. "Have you ever considered that he deserves a good life? A life that he chooses for himself? What makes you think he deserves to be married to someone who is like you—a sad, pathetic, manipulative, heartless, selfish, backstabbing shrew!"

Edwin Sr. stepped past his son and looked at his wife. "Myra, you should be ashamed! But my guess is that you are not. I've been telling you for years to leave him alone. But you wouldn't listen. I knew that you were a heartless user but I never would have thought that you would go so far as to deliberately ruin your son's relationship just to get your way."

Joshua didn't want to be insolent, but he felt compelled to let his mother know what her actions had done to him. "Mother, I've held my tongue over the years out of respect for you, but I have to say that your most recent treacherous actions have caused me deep pain. I told you before how I feel. You were never a caring mother until I was old enough to take care of myself and didn't need you anymore. There was always something else for you to do, or somewhere you had to go. The nanny showed me more love than my own mother."

He dropped his hands, stood behind Finell, and rested his hands on her still trembling shoulders.

"I love this woman completely," Joshua continued, "and I'm going to spend the rest of my life with her. And there is nothing you can say or do that will make me change my mind."

Joshua shifted so that he was now standing in front of Finell. She had her arms around his waist and her head rested on his back.

"I would like to say that I want nothing else to do with you ever again," Joshua went on, "but you're my mother and I have to respect you as such. However, if you and I never speak again, it will be too soon for me." He looked at his father and his uncle and asked, "Would you please get them out of my house?"

Edwin Sr. stepped to his wife, took her arm, and walked her out of the apartment as Irvin Sr. and a still-crying Marlee followed.

"Myra," Edwin Sr. said, "this time for sure I know you've lost your son's loyalty. I don't believe he'll ever forgive you for this."

EJ looked at his brother and then let his eyes rest on Finell. "Be happy, you two," he said with a wink, then walked out, closing the door behind himself.

When the door closed, Joshua and Finell dropped to the sofa with arms entangled. After wiping her tears, Joshua said, "There are so many reasons why I love you. One of those reasons was demonstrated here tonight. You had my back, didn't you?"

Finell offered him a watery smile. "I'm going to try to always have your back. I'm so very much in love with you, Mr. Hamilton."

After kissing her to the point where they both almost lost control, they prayed together and he drove her home.

The next morning, Joshua picked up Finell and they rode to work together. The events of the previous night had seemed to bond them closer together.

As they stepped off the elevator, Joshua walked to the break room to get his cup of coffee and her cup of tea. Mrs. Mimms followed Finell into her office and smiled at the younger woman. "I saw you two arrive together this morning. What's going on? Did you spend the night with our boss?"

Joshua stepped thru the door and set Finell's cup on her desk. "Good morning, Mrs. Mimms," he said with a scowl of disapproval. "I believe we have some statistical reports to review this morning. I'll see you in my office in five minutes."

Slightly embarrassed at being caught trying to get some inside gossip, Mrs. Mimms scurried out to her desk.

As he was leaving, Joshua looked back at Finell, smiled his award-winning smile, and said, "I got your back too, babe."

Looking at her with a deep love shining in his eyes, Joshua smiled and walked out of her office.

CHAPTER 10

David Colwins had been hearing rumors that Finell was engaged to her boss and was determined not to believe it until he heard it from her.

On Wednesday evening after prayer service, Joshua and Finell were having their usual midweek dinner date. The atmosphere was pensive. Joshua was going out of town to attend some seminars at the seminary where he was studying to receive his Masters of Divinity.

Finell was trying to be upbeat about the separation. "I'm going to miss you, but I pray that the seminars are uplifting."

"Oh, they will be very interesting and informative, but I'm going to miss seeing you," Joshua said. "Don't forget that I'm going to try and call you every evening after our last class. If I can't call, I'll text you a quick message."

Thursday was the first day that Joshua was gone, and getting through the day was a long, lonely ordeal. As she was driving home, Finell smiled to herself and thought, *At least Mom and Dad are at the house. I'll be glad to have some company tonight.*

It helped that her parents were still with her and gave her some comfort when she arrived home. While they had dinner together,

Finell talked about her day at work and about how much she missed Joshua. After dinner, they watched the evening news and Finell said goodnight to her parents, went to her bedroom, climbed into her bed, and slept until her phone chimed that she had received a text message.

Hey, beautiful. Lots of homework. Miss you. Love you. God bless and keep you. Your man, JH

On Friday evening after work, as she was walking to her car, Finell saw a bouquet of roses sitting on the roof. Opening the door, she threw her purse and briefcase in before she lifted the flowers from the top of the car.

The card read: *Hello 'Nell. These are for you. I hope you still like roses. Enjoy. I love you.*

She looked up and saw David standing on the passenger side of her car. "You are so beautiful. I know I should have said it more when we were together. But if you give me another chance, I promise to say it a lot. We were good together, 'Nell, and we can be even better this time."

"David," she said, "I'm getting married soon, and—"

Before she could say more, David interrupted. "So? I'm already married. That shouldn't keep us apart. I want you. I never should have let you go. What I did was foolish, it was all about sex. But what you and I had was love. I want that again."

She looked at him and wanted to throw the flowers in his face, but she thought it would be best if she tried to reason with him. "David, you need to understand that it's too late for you and me. I don't love you. As a matter of fact, I don't think that I ever loved you. There will never be a you and me ever again. You did me a favor when you left me. Let's just leave things the way they are right now."

Looking at her like she was speaking a foreign language, David said, "I know you were mad at me back then, but you can't still be mad at me, baby. I made a mistake. Stop playing with me. We need to be back together again."

"Listen carefully to me," Finell said, "I love Joshua very much, and he loves me. There's no place in our lives for anyone else." She threw the flowers across the roof of her car, jumped in, and locked the doors. She cranked the engine and pulled away from David and his crazy ideas. She drove as quickly as she could without breaking the speed limit and kept looking in her rearview mirror to be sure he wasn't following her.

She sighed deeply. *He must be crazy. I was saved from making the biggest mistake of my life. I've been blessed to have the love of a man who is honest and trustworthy. I'm not going to do anything to destroy that blessing.* The encounter with David had shaken her confidence, and she tried to recover her spirits. *Joshua Hamilton is the most wonderful thing that has happened to me in my life. There's no way that David Colwins could ever measure up to my Joshua.*

She thought about calling Joshua when she got home to tell him what had just happened, but she didn't want to worry him. "Besides," she said aloud to herself, "there's nothing he can do from where he is anyway."

She ate dinner with her parents, watched the news with them again, then went to her room, showered, and went to bed. She lay there until her phone chimed, alerting her to a new text.

Sweetheart, lots of homework again tonight. I miss your voice, your beautiful face, and that warm body. Can't hardly wait for the next three weeks to pass and you'll be mine. Love you. God bless you. Your man, JH.

The next morning as she was getting ready to leave for work, Finell heard the doorbell ring. Her mother answered, and when Finell got there, she saw a car backing out of the driveway and several bouquets of roses on the front step.

"Mom," she asked, "who was that so early in the morning?"

Karina picked up the flowers and brought them inside. "Well, I don't know who they were," she said, "but they left roses. Aren't they beautiful?" She looked through the flowers and found the accompanying card. "Who are they from?"

"Enjoy them," Finell said. "They're most likely from Daddy."

"Hold up a minute, young lady," Karina said with an edge to her voice. "These are for you. And you can wipe that grin off your face because they're not from Joshua."

Finell took the card and read the message: *You'll be mine again. I love you, David.* She recoiled and dropped the card. "Throw those things away," she said, beside herself with anger, shaking her hands like she'd just touched something nasty. "That man must be out of his mind. Throw them away. Eww!"

"What is this all about?" Karina asked.

"I'll tell you when I get home tonight. Don't worry, it's nothing," she said and picked up her bags.

She walked into her garage, pressed the garage door remote, got in her car, and drove to work, grumbling, "David Colwins is a pest! Why did I ever think that I wanted to be married to him?"

She shook her head.

"Because you were pitiful and pathetic," she answered herself admonishingly. "David is what happens when you pray for something then go out and find it yourself instead of waiting for God to answer your prayers." She shivered. "Thank you, Lord, for rescuing me from myself."

* * *

The week after Joshua returned from the seminary, Finell walked into his office and tentatively asked, "Is this a good time for you to talk?"

"I always have time for you," he said. "What's up?"

She told him, "I've been praying about us and our future together, and I don't think we will be very happy as long as you and your mother are estranged. After all, she is your mother, and I'm sure that you would want her to attend our wedding."

Joshua stood slowly and walked from his desk to the windows. Finell felt a shift within but didn't know what to do. After several minutes, Joshua turned and looked at her with an expression she had never seen before.

"I don't think the situation between me and my mother is any of your business," he said. He stood tall with his hands shoved deep in his pockets and his eyes boring into hers. His chest was rising and falling, and his breathing escalated as though he were trying to control his temper.

Finell was shocked by the level of vehemence in his voice, and she stepped back from the spark of intensity in his eyes. "I don't want you to think that I'm prying into your personal business," she said, "but my concern is for you. You are unhappy, and it makes me hurt for you."

"Well, don't do that! I'm fine, and I'll deal with my mother when I get good and ready to deal with her. Leave it alone, Finell, please!"

Her feelings hurt, she turned and left his office. He had never treated her that way. *Lord*, she prayed, *I beg your forgiveness for stepping out of line and not allowing you to handle this situation. I love him, and I don't want to see him in conflict. He's hurting, and you're the only one who can relieve his pain. I ask that you soothe him and comfort him at this time. In Your Son's name, I pray. Amen.*

Joshua looked at the closed door and breathed in deeply, pulling in the sweet, lingering scent of the woman he dearly loved. "I'm sorry, babe. I didn't mean to hurt you," he whispered.

Picking up his desk telephone, he dialed his father.

"Dad," he said, "I think I just messed up big time. I need to talk to you. Can we meet?"

At lunch, Joshua walked the four blocks to the Good Eats Café and looked around for his father. Not much to his surprise, he saw that Alphonso Everson was with him. The two men had become fast friends since the family dinner at the hotel well over a month earlier. The three men greeted one another and shook hands, then gave the waitress their food and drink orders before they settled down to discuss Joshua's situation.

"So," Mr. Everson said, "what's going on, young man? Your father informs me that you only call him during this time of day when there's a problem. I hope the problem is not my daughter."

With eyes downcast, Joshua said, "There is a problem, but it's not *with* your daughter. It's *because* of your daughter."

His future father-in-law's eyebrows rose, and he leaned forward. "Continue, son, this sounds interesting."

"Dad," Joshua said, "Mr. Everson. I've been praying about the situation between me and Mom. I haven't spoken to her since that night at my apartment. Ever since then, God has been urging me to breach the gap and contact her so that we can meet and straighten things out. But I've been putting it off."

"So how does Finell figure into this thing, son?" Mr. Everson asked.

"This morning, Fin came into my office and told me she had been praying about the same situation, and she suggested the same thing that I've been urged to do. I wasn't ready to hear her say that, and I reacted in a way that I'm sure hurt her feelings."

"So, what happened when you apologized?" Mr. Everson asked.

Before he could answer, Edwin Sr. spoke up. "He hasn't

apologized yet. Have you son?"

Sighing heavily, Joshua shook his head. "I don't know how."

Laughing, the two men offered their suggestions. "Sincerely," Mr. Hamilton advised, while Mr. Everson declared, "And with a nice gift." Both men laughed again when they saw the confusion on Joshua's face.

Alphonso Everson softly asserted, "Son, for future reference, you should know that a good husband listens to his wife. He should never have a negative reaction to anything his wife says. Your job, Joshua, is to listen carefully, then use non-judgmental words when you do find it necessary to respond."

Smiling, Edwin Hamilton suggested, "Let's have our lunch so you can stop somewhere to get that nice gift before you return to your office to *sincerely* apologize."

* * *

Having skipped lunch to complete some reports that Joshua had asked the supervisors to turn in by the end of the week, Finell wanted to get her department's report in early. As she was leaving her office to make some copies, she ran into Mrs. Mimms carrying a blue-etched crystal vase filled with a large bouquet of pink and purple daisy poms. They were mixed with mini carnations, asters, and Peruvian lilies. "These are for you. Aren't they beautiful?" Mrs. Mimms gushed as she handed them to Finell.

Just then, Joshua stepped off the elevator. "Read the card," he said.

She did. Then she looked up, turned her back to him, set the vase down, and wrapped her arms around her waist. Joshua put his hands on his fiancée's shoulders and turned her around to face him.

"I'm so very sorry," he said. "You were absolutely right, but I let my male ego get in the way. I hope that you can forgive me for what I said and how I said it."

He unwrapped her hands and kissed the insides of her wrists, then he moved his arms to wrap them around her waist, pulled her close, and kissed her. As he felt the tension in her body subside, he deepened the kiss, and they didn't part until they heard clapping.

"Alright, alright, don't you people have better things to do than watch these two lovebirds?" Mrs. Mimms said to the office workers who had gathered to watch their boss make his moves. "Show's over, everyone. Get back to work." Then, looking at her boss with one hand on her hip, she pointed to the vase. "I assume these are for Miss Everson, so if you want you, can carry them into her office for her. That way, you can both make a clean getaway and have some privacy."

As the couple followed her suggestion, Mrs. Mimms smiled and nodded her head.

"Now, *that's* how a man ought to apologize."

* * *

After work, Finell ran a few errands before she went home. Pulling into the driveway of the house that in two weeks would no longer be her home, she pressed the garage door remote and saw her parents and fiancé standing inside.

Her father walked to her side of the car. "Hey, little girl! Leave the car on. Your mom and I are going for a ride. Joshua has something to say to you."

After Joshua lifted the big vase of flowers from the back seat of Finell's car, the two stepped back and watched her parents drive away.

NIGHTMARE

Inside, Joshua set the bouquet in the middle of the kitchen table while Finell washed her hands and began putting their place settings on the table. Whatever her mother had cooked smelled temptingly delicious.

When they were finally sitting down to eat, Joshua said, "You were right, Fin. There's a real need to clear the air between me and my mother. So I called her and told her we were coming over. When we finish eating and cleaning the kitchen, I want us to go to my parents' house."

Joshua prayed for peace and understanding as they drove to the home he was raised in. Once they arrived, he took Finell's elbow and led her to the front door.

Myra was anxiously awaiting her son's arrival, but she wasn't expecting to see Finell, and because of that, she wasn't able to keep the surprise from showing on her face. Ringing in her ear was her husband's warning that if she offended Joshua or Finell in any way, she should be prepared to not be invited to the wedding. Still not believing that she'd been out of line, Myra intended to heed her husband's warning. At least this time.

"Thanks for making time to talk to us, Mother," Joshua said and kissed Myra's cheek. "I'm here because Finell doesn't want us to get married with divisions in the family. I want you to know that she wants us to talk and maybe start a move toward forgiveness.."

When his mother gasped, pulled a handkerchief from her sleeve, and dabbed her eyes, Joshua tried hard not to lose patience.

"I just hope you will make up your mind that Finell and I are getting married and there's nothing you can do to hinder that."

Myra's eyes shifted from her son's handsome face to the face of the woman he was holding fast to his side. "How nice of you to think of me," she said, "but it's really my place to apologize to you. I'm sorry for my actions. Please know, however, that whatever I do in relation to my son is because I love him."

Knowing that what had just transpired between them was probably as good as it was going to get, Finell stood from the couch and walked out of the formal living room. She felt Joshua behind her, and when she stopped on the landing just outside the front door, he pulled her back to his chest, leaned forward, and smiled against her ear.

"Are you satisfied now?" he asked.

When she laughed and nodded her head, he kissed her on the shoulder. With shivers running rampant through her body, she laughed, "You need to stop that or else I'm going to ravage your body right here in front of this house for the whole world to see."

Joshua stepped around her and took her hand. Grinning, he said, "Promises, promises."

CHAPTER 11

The day of Joshua and Finell's wedding finally arrived.
The ceremony was filled with pomp and circumstance. Pastor Benson officiated over the ceremony, working hard to make everything special so that the couple would never forget it. And while it was an unforgettable event surrounded by loved ones and supporters, the bride and groom would only remember looking into each other's eyes, anxiously awaiting the moment when the pastor spoke the words that finally bound them together forever: "I now pronounce you husband and wife." And then came the words that followed: "Joshua Hamilton, salute your bride."

Finell was overjoyed to be Mrs. Joshua Hamilton. As Joshua looked down into the eyes of the woman he dearly and deeply loved, his thoughts revolved around the task before them—the task of blending their lives, starting with tonight when they would join their bodies together, becoming one in heart, mind, body, and soul.

After the ceremony, during the reception when they stood in the middle of the dance floor staring into each other's eyes, Finell asked, "What are you thinking about, Mr. Hamilton?"

"You, my beautiful bride. You and me and us," he answered as he gathered her closer.

Just as he was about to lower his head to kiss his wife, Joshua felt a hand on his shoulder. "Hey, little brother, did you two forget that you are in a room full of church people? Listen, before you start the honeymoon right here and now, why don't you let me dance with my new sister-in-law?" Mindful of his brother's ever-watchful eyes on him, a smiling EJ pulled Finell into a loose embrace, knowing his brother was hovering over them. "I still think that you should have married me, girl," he said teasingly, waggling his eyebrows.

Finell shook his arms and laughed as they danced away from Joshua. EJ's tone grew serious when he continued, "I love my brother, and I'm happy for him. He's waited a long time for a wife, and I'm so glad that it's you. I hope you two will be happy for the rest of your lives together. Congratulations."

As the music ended, he kissed her on the cheek, folded her hand over his arm, and walked her back to her husband. Releasing Finell's hand, EJ stepped to his brother and said, "I'm proud of you, Josh. I want the two of you to be happy forever. Okay?"

The brothers hugged and kissed each other's cheeks, and when they stepped back, they both punched the other in his chest and smiled.

Myra Hamilton was seated at the parents' table. She was tired of smiling her false smile, accepting congratulations, and pretending to be happy that her child had married into a family that was not even on her social register.

* * *

Finally, the reception was over and the eager couple left the banquet room of the hotel through a barrage of bubbles.

NIGHTMARE

Joshua led his new bride to his car, helped her in, and as they drove away, he said, "Well, my dear Mrs. Hamilton, how are you feeling?"

Beaming, Finell replied, "I can't say how I feel right now. So much is going on. I'm excited. I'm happy. I'm a little anxious, but mostly, I'm curious about where we're going."

Joshua chuckled softly as he replied, "Oh, not very far. Just trust me and lay your head back, close your eyes, and I'll let you know when we get to our destination."

After a thirty-minute drive, Joshua made a sharp turn and pulled into the driveway of a house with a semi-circular driveway and a three-car garage. He touched Finell's hand and gave it a light squeeze. "Okay, Mrs. Hamilton," he said joyously, "you can wake up. We're here."

"Where are we?"

"Our home for the next fifty to sixty years," he said affectionately as he exited the car. Instead of pulling into the garage, he had driven the car around the driveway to the front door. He helped Finell from the car, and hand in hand they walked up the three semi-circular steps to the landing that led to the house's double-door entry.

Joshua shook his key ring and selected a shiny gold key, inserted it into the deadbolt, unlocked it, and pushed the doors open as far as they would go. Next, he lifted his wife into his arms and stepped across the threshold.

"Welcome home, Finell," he said. "I pray that we are happy here together for a very long time. I know that it's a big house, but I want us to fill it up with lots of fun, laughter, love, and children."

Joshua kissed her and then set her back on her feet.

"This was my grandparents' first home," he told her. "They sold it to me five years ago for $100 and moved to California. EJ and I have been working on it for two years. I hope you like it."

Finell looked around. They stood in the middle of the entry hall with a bright, highly polished golden oak hardwood floor and a framed bay window with a deep and wide golden oak window seat. To Finell, the room was enchanting.

After closing the doors, Joshua took her hand. "Let me give you a tour."

They walked straight ahead and down three steps. To the left was the living room. That room was empty except for a recliner, a sixty-five-inch flat-screen television on an entertainment cabinet, and a table with a lamp and a large multi-use remote control resting on it.

Walking through the living room, they entered a hallway that led to a den on the left and the dining room on the right. Instead of walking through the formal dining room, they continued down the hallway and entered the kitchen.

Finell stood in the doorway and looked around the kitchen. It was a large room, and it too had a bay window that cradled a breakfast nook. Set in the wall beside the bay window, she saw a set of double-wide French doors leading to the backyard. Across the expanse of the kitchen was the door to the laundry room. Next to the laundry room was a servant's quarters bedroom and bathroom with a shower. Those rooms were near the door that led from the garage to the house, all connected by a common hallway.

Finell grinned at the realization that the kitchen, equipped with all-new black stainless-steel appliances, was the only other room on the first floor that was completely furnished—if you could call a card table and four folding chairs furniture.

As they stood holding hands and looking around, Joshua laughed. "Don't look so forlorn. We're both on vacation for a week, and we can use some of that time to shop for furniture."

NIGHTMARE

The newly joined Mr. and Mrs. Hamilton turned around and went back to the entry hall. To the right was a staircase that led to the second floor where the master suite, three other bedrooms, and two more full bathrooms were located.

The only room with furniture on this level was the master suite, and it was richly decorated. The bedroom contained a large walk-in dressing closet and a massive oak four-poster king-size bed. Finell was glad to see that there was a step stool on one side of the bed. The rest of the expansive room contained a double dresser with a mirror, a triple wardrobe, a six-drawer lingerie bureau, and a double chest of drawers that all matched the bed.

"You have good taste, Mr. Hamilton," Finell said, flashing a wide smile at her husband.

Joshua thought, *My wife is the most beautiful woman that I have ever seen.* He realized at that moment that he loved her with a love that was so deep and pure that all he wanted to do was to protect her from the evils of this world. He wanted to be one with her; to see, hear, taste, and touch her and only her as his lifetime mate. Joshua was sure at this very moment that no other woman would ever take her place in his heart.

Finell walked through the room, touching each piece of furniture. She stepped into the walk-in closet and saw that one side was filled and the other side was almost completely empty. She called out, "I'm guessing this is my side of the closet. How did some of my clothes get here?"

Joshua stepped to her and wrapped her in his loving embrace. "Yes, Mrs. Hamilton, this is your half of the closet, just like everything that I have and every place in this house. Earlier this week, I asked your mother and your sister to bring over some things for you to wear after the wedding."

"Well. You thought about clothes and shoes, but did you think about underwear?" she asked.

Walking to the tall, narrow dresser on her side of the room, Joshua slid open several of the drawers. "Your mother and sister did."

"Then I guess I should thank them, especially since everything in these drawers appears to be brand new," she said, looking at the items in the dresser. Turning to hug Joshua, Finell said, "But first, I think I should thank you for being so thoughtful." Rising on her toes, she kissed his cheek.

"Oh, you can thank me better than that, can't you?" Joshua pulled her even closer and reached for the zipper of her dress. "Let's get ready for bed," he whispered.

When he stepped back, Finell's dress fell to the floor and pooled at her feet, leaving her standing in her white lace bra, matching panties, garter belt, and stockings. Her arms moved up to cover her body, but Joshua engulfed her hands in his and gently moved them down to her sides.

"You don't have to be shy with me," he said, "or hide yourself from me, ever. I love you and everything about you. Never be ashamed about anything, especially when we are together. You are a wonderfully made creation. And I love everything about you. Everything."

To make her feel even more comfortable, Joshua let his jacket slide off his shoulders and dropped it on the floor. He removed articles of clothing until he was standing in nothing but his t-shirt, mid-thigh briefs, and trouser socks.

"Well, then," Finell said suggestively, "let's take a shower and we can go to bed."

While Finell was showering, Joshua went to one of the guest rooms and showered. When she stepped back into the bedroom wrapped in a bath sheet, he returned to the room with a towel around his waist.

With a suddenly dry mouth, Finell tried to swallow but couldn't. The man standing before her had a mesmerizing body—a well-defined chest, toned arms, strong legs, and a six-pack.

She jumped. "Oh, no. I didn't want you to see me like this! I forgot my lingerie."

Walking to where she was standing, Joshua raised his hands and cupped her face, lowered his head, and kissed her tenderly, starting with her temples, her forehead, her eyes, her cheeks, and then her beautiful, soft, full lips. With each kiss, he whispered, "I love you."

When the kissing ended, he unwrapped her towel, pulled her close, and held her to his body. They stood locked together until their hearts were beating in unison.

She listened to his heart beat, absorbed his body heat, smelled his woodsy, musky scent, and at that moment, she accepted that he was her lover, her protector, and her husband. She whispered, "Thank you, Lord."

Joshua felt her warm, smooth skin under his hands and smelled her sweet, soft lavender chamomile scent as she slowly slid her arms around his waist, bringing them even closer. Pressed against his body, her breasts awakened sensations that he had no idea could be so intense. The pressure caused his body to have reactions that could only be quelled in one way, and one way only. And he was more than ready.

Leaning back, Joshua looked down into Finell's alluring eyes. He could feel the anxiety and trepidation building within her. Smiling sensuously, he said, "Babe, it's time for us to begin our journey into the world of marriage. Are you ready?"

Nodding her head, Finell softly said, "Yes, I'm ready."

The journey began with them walking across the room and falling into the bed as they began exploring each other's bodies by taste, touch, scent, sound, and sight until they connected their emotions by becoming as close as two people can get.

They spent the rest of the night in the euphoria of discovering each other. Because they were both sharing their first lovemaking experience, they had a very enjoyable and exploratory first night in their marriage bed.

Finell was curious but afraid.

Joshua was anxious, patient, and gentle, but hungry.

Both realized that love was not just a pleasurable physical experience but a journey of the heart, mind, body, and soul.

Eventually, they tired and fell asleep, happily wrapped in each other's arms.

* * *

Finell was in the twilight stage of sleep. She heard herself moan, and when she opened her eyes, she realized she had good reason to do so. Her husband was hovering over her, and his hands and mouth were gently roaming, nipping, and nuzzling her body.

"Are you going to wake me up every morning like this?" she asked sweetly.

"Yes, definitely. That is, unless you want to flip the script on me one morning."

"Oh, you can count on it."

They hugged each other close as they laughed.

A little while later, Joshua and Finell reluctantly rolled out of bed. When they entered the bathroom, the tub was filled with warm water and fragranced by a green tea and waterlily bath oil.

"I left the tub heater on so that the water would be warm to help sooth you," Joshua said.

As he helped her step into the tub, Finell said, "You are full of wonderful surprises, Mr. Hamilton. Thank you for being so thoughtful."

"I knew you would be sore, so I thought this would help."

"Come in with me," she said, still holding his hand.

He looked at her. "Stop tempting me like that, Mrs. Finell Hamilton. I can't join you in there because I don't want to hurt you. Besides, we have a lot to do today." He reluctantly stepped into the shower as she soaked her sore body in the tub.

After breakfast, the newlyweds began their first day of marriage by driving to Finell's house to pick up the rest of her clothes, shoes, and other necessary items. When they arrived, Karina Everson watched as her new son-in-law helped his wife from the truck. They stepped slowly together, embracing and kissing as only newlyweds do.

"Rina, what's so interesting?" Mr. Everson asked as he stepped behind his wife and settled his hands on her shoulders. "Oh, I see!"

With all the looking that was going on, no one noticed the car that had been backed into the neighbor's driveway across the street. Nor did they notice who was seated behind the wheel.

David Colwins smirked. "Well, isn't that cute!" Then his expression hardened. "He'd better enjoy all of that now because she's mine, and I intend to let her know that beyond a shadow of a doubt."

He started the car and slowly rolled out of the driveway and down the street, undetected by anyone.

After Joshua's truck had been loaded and Finell had given her parents the new deed to the house with their names on it, she and Joshua drove back to 5995 Old Green Springs Lane. They spent the rest of the morning and part of the afternoon unpacking boxes and putting things in place, changing his bedroom into their bedroom.

After sitting up late that night making a list of what they needed to do to make the house their home, the couple started the next day with the task of shopping for furniture, rugs, curtains, and other items to turn their house into a comfortable place to call home.

They went to the Furniture Galleria, a store located in an upscale mall on the outskirts of the city's business district.

Before they exited the car, Joshua said, "Well, here we are, let's get busy."

"Is this where we're going to buy our furniture?" Finell asked.

"Yes, and most of everything else that we need. Why? Is there a problem?"

"No, there's no problem. What's our budget?"

"Don't worry about it. Just get what you like."

"No! I want to stay within a price range that we can afford."

Joshua raised his hands in surrender. "Look, babe, it's okay. I like this store, and I like the furniture they sell. It's where I got the bedroom set. And you do like the bedroom set, don't you?"

She swatted his hand. "Yes, but..." She huffed. "This place is very expensive, Josh. I don't want us to get too deep in debt and possibly lose everything."

"Are we having our first argument?" Joshua jokingly asked, but before she could answer, he took her hands. "Our budget is between $100,000 to $250,000. We are going to furnish almost the whole house. We have the entire downstairs and the three guest bedrooms upstairs to furnish, plus the family and entertainment rooms in the basement."

She looked at him and sighed. "I don't want you to have to work for years to pay off this debt. We can always get new furniture, but I can't get another you."

Joshua opened his door, stepped out of the car, and as he was helping her out of the passenger side, he lifted her chin with his finger. "Don't worry. We have enough money to get what we need and want."

"I'm sure we can do this if you say so," Finell said, relenting. "I have a savings account and the money my parents gave me for my house. I'm sure we'll have more than enough for a good down payment."

"Babe," Joshua said, calling her by his favorite love name and lifting her chin a little higher, "I know we have enough money even without your savings, because…well…I'm a multimillionaire."

Her eyes grew big. *"What?"*

He slowly nodded his head.

"Nooo," she almost moaned.

Appearing amused, he said, "It's true. I'm a little more well off than the average person my age."

"Why? Why didn't you tell me before now?" She stepped away from him and walked over to stand by the front bumper of the car. "Joshua Hamilton, if you had told me sooner, we could have eliminated this whole conversation and I wouldn't be feeling like I'm going to pass out right about now."

When he walked up to her and opened his arms, she pushed him in the chest before she hugged him. "No wonder your mother thought I was after you for your money. Joshua, you should have told me. You are such a mess."

He looked at her and raised an eyebrow. "Well, would that have made a difference to you?"

"Of course," she said, laughing. "I would have made you chase me a little harder. I don't want you thinking you can get any woman you want just because you're a little better off than other men your age."

His mouth dropped open, and they both laughed. "I love you,

Mrs. Hamilton," Joshua said, "and if you want me to, I'll give every dime I have away. Just to make you happy."

"You better not. You earned what you have. All I ask is that you not keep any more major secrets from me."

"That's a promise, my beautiful bride."

Finell would never have suspected Joshua was wealthy. He was such a modest, self-contained, down-to-earth, austere man that she didn't have a clue that he had what he called "a few million."

He explained to her that his grandparents had given him a one-million-dollar trust fund at birth, and when he graduated from college, they increased it by another two million. She learned that he was financially savvy and had never spent more than one-third of his yearly salary since he began working at USI. He owned the apartment building that he lived in, as well as several others downtown. He had recently stopped rolling the interest from his trust back into the fund account, and had it transferred to his expense account at his bank, which now also had his wife's name on it.

CHAPTER 12

Two weeks before the wedding, David Colwins heard about it through a friend that attended the God Samaritan Church where Finell was now a member. That explained why he hadn't seen her at the church she used to make him attend when they were engaged. Most of all, he didn't want to believe she was really getting married to Joshua Hamilton.

"Married?" he exclaimed lightly to his friend. "You mean that the poor desperate sucker is actually going to marry my reject?"

He thought that by saying such disparaging things no one would ever know he felt like he'd made a mistake by not marrying Finell. He realized too late that he did more than "kinda" love her. Yeah, she was a big girl, but she was still pretty. All you had to do was look at her pictures in the magazines and catalogs to see her beauty.

David was now thinking more and more of himself as a fool because he'd let her get away. And he had no idea she was engaged. He just thought she had been playing hard to get. So he began to drive through her neighborhood every day on his way to work and on his way home. For a couple of weeks, he would even drive past the house on weekends.

His feelings became more and more intense because he wanted

to talk to her, not realizing he was already too late. One day, as he drove past, he saw the couple embracing in the driveway of 1977 Laramore Drive.

It was at that time that David formulated his plan to make Finell part of his life again. He convinced himself that he could persuade her to change her mind and get back with him.

I know it's not too late, he thought. *She can't still be mad. I know she still loves me. This new guy is just a replacement for me. All I have to do is let her know again that even though I'm married, she and I can still be together.*

After he was told that she was getting married, David decided to step up his plan to get back together with her. He decided to become more visible to her. He was determined to wear her down and make her see things his way. He called her home number the following Monday evening, but he discovered her landline was no longer in service. When he drove by the house, he didn't see her car, but that didn't mean much because she made it a habit to always park inside the garage. When he called her cell phone, she let him go to voicemail.

"Finell," he'd demanded, "you need to answer my calls!"

His next call on Tuesday evening was not so demanding. "Hey, 'Nell. It's me again. Call me back, I want to talk to you. It's important."

On Wednesday morning, he'd said, "You need to stop playing with me, 'Nell. You know who this is and you know what I want. Meet me at our favorite spot by 7:30 tonight. I can't wait to see you. I've missed you."

By Thursday afternoon, David was determined to talk to her so he started calling every hour until she picked up his call. A week later, after he had driven past Finell's house again and saw her kissing that guy, David decided he was going to call her cell number every hour until she answered the phone.

NIGHTMARE

She needs to know that I'm serious about us being back together again.

Joshua heard Finell's phone buzzing in her purse. "Fin, your phone is buzzing. It's been doing it every hour. Someone really wants to speak with you." He carried the satchel to the kitchen and set it on the end of the counter.

"I'm busy with dinner right now," Finell said. "Can you get it for me, please?"

Joshua answered and a voice on the other end said, "I called to speak to Finell. Why are you answering her phone?"

"Speak to her about what?"

"None of your business, church boy. Give the phone to my 'Nell!" David demanded. "I've been leaving her flowers and messages, but I guess you've been in her face so much that she hasn't had time to listen to them and get back to me."

Finell could tell by her husband's expression that the caller was being rude.

"It would be in your best interest if you stopped calling this number," Joshua said just before he threw the phone across the room. When it hit the wall, it left a dent and shattered into pieces. "Why didn't you tell me that he was calling you again?" Joshua demanded.

"Who?" Finell asked, looking at him with wide eyes.

"Who? You have the nerve to ask me who. Colwins, that's who!"

"Because I never took his calls."

"But you took the flowers!"

"I have not taken *anything* from David Colwins! The last time I saw him, I told him that my heart belonged to you. I rejected his advances and his flowers. And told him that without a doubt there will never, ever again be a him and me."

"*Saw him?*" Joshua exploded. "You *saw* him? Have you been

meeting with him?"

Realizing that her husband was upset, Finell focused on Joshua as she told him about the flowers on her car and the ones left on her doorstep.

"Why didn't you tell me?" he asked again, his voice booming and his body rigid.

"You were taking the classes at the seminary. What could you have done? You weren't here. I felt like I could handle the situation myself. I haven't seen him since that day, and like I just told you, I have been ignoring his calls. He just started that calling-every-hour thing. I was going to block his number, but I forgot. Every time I do block him, he gets a new number."

With flared nostrils, he threw out, "We're changing your number immediately!"

"While you're doing that, you need to get me a new phone, too."

Joshua blinked his eyes and shook his head. "This is not the time to play with me!" He banged his fist on the counter. "You should have told me!"

Finell jumped, then stared at him but said nothing. He could tell that he'd frightened her, but he didn't care.

"I don't like him having access to you. I don't like it one bit! You need to remember that you are *my wife*, and he needs to be made to respect that!"

Finell washed and dried her hands, threw the towel on the counter, and with misty eyes poked him in his chest. "Well, I don't like it either, but what I like the least right now is your attitude. That man is not part of my life anymore. As a matter of fact, I wish he had never been in the first place." She took a deep breath, put her hands flat on his chest, and continued. "You are my husband. I know that beyond a shadow of a doubt, and I love you dearly. I will never give you a reason to doubt my loyalty or my love."

Pushing away from him, she stormed out of the kitchen with her chin up, her back straight, and her shoulders squared.

When his breathing slowed down and his anger dissipated to a point where he could think coherently, Joshua turned off the stove and went looking for his wife. Kicking off his shoes, he climbed onto the bed behind Finell. He kissed the back of her neck as he spooned her.

"I'm sorry," he said. "I didn't mean for you to think that I don't trust you. It's just that I don't like him, and I especially don't like the way he keeps popping up in our lives. He could become dangerous, and if he hurts you, I'm going to have to kill him."

Finell turned to face Joshua so that she could look at his handsome face. "Let's let the law handle David Colwins. The man is like a nightmare—popping up at the wrong times, invading my peace of mind, and becoming very aggravatingly and disturbingly unwelcome. I realized while you were gone that if I didn't do something, he was not ever going to accept the fact that I'm never going to let him back into my life. So I had a restraining order drawn up against him." She caressed Joshua's cheek. "Don't let his behavior draw you away from God's plan for you…for us."

Joshua raised his hand and slowly wiped the tears from Finell's cheeks. "I'm sorry I let my temper get out of control. But when it comes to you, I'm very protective." He leaned closer and gently kissed the tear tracks on her cheeks.

"How sorry are you?" she asked.

Pulling back, he frowned at her. "I'll get you a new phone."

Chuckling, Finell replied, "I don't care about the phone. I want to know if you are *really* sorry." She smiled suggestively and pressed her body close to his as she slid her hands under his shirt to rub his chest.

Joshua kissed her passionately. "Oh, I am really, *really* sorry. Let me prove to you just how sorry I am."

An hour after their argument, they returned to the kitchen to finish cooking and have their dinner.

* * *

When David dialed Finell's number the next day, he received a voice message that said, "The number you are trying to reach is no longer in service."

"So he wants to play hardball," he said to himself. "I know that he's the one who changed her number. But that won't keep me away from her. If he thinks so, then he has seriously underestimated me."

On a Friday morning two months after their wedding, Finell was preparing to leave home and drive to Parker City for the quarterly evaluations. She was at the mirror tying a scarf around her neck after trying to cover the passion bruises with makeup when Joshua came up behind her, kissed her behind the ear, and nuzzled down her neck to her shoulder.

As he expected, she laughed and wiggled against him. "Josh, behave yourself. I'm trying to get ready for work. And I don't need another one of your *love notes* anywhere else on my body."

He smiled against her shoulder. "So do you think they'll get the message when they look at you?"

She turned to face him and put her arms around his neck. She kissed him and said, "And if they don't get the visual hint, then I'll be more than glad to give them a verbal one."

Thirty minutes later, after taking another shower and changing clothes again, they were both headed out the front door of their home.

"I'm sorry we didn't have time for breakfast," Joshua said as he helped her into her car, and handed her a granola bar and her insulated cup of tea. After they prayed, he said, "Be careful. Drive safe. I'll see you this afternoon. I love you."

"I love you, too," she replied as she pulled around the driveway and down the street toward the freeway.

* * *

David Colwins was getting desperate. He needed to talk to Finell. He wanted to make sure she knew that he was willing to restart their relationship.

She needs to know that she doesn't have to be with that Hamilton guy anymore, he thought. *I just want to tell her that we are a couple again. And she needs to know that no piece of paper will keep me away from her!*

David went to his office and worked feverishly all morning so that he could finish the work that was still on his desk. All the while, his mind was on Finell. As much as he hated to disturb her at work, he felt she didn't leave him any other choice. He planned to go to her office and take her to lunch. He had to convince her that she should be with him and not Joshua Hamilton.

He thought there was never any better time than right now. Especially now that Abigail was gone. Abigail had been home the day the police had delivered the restraining order. As a result, she was angry, demanding to know why Finell Everson had to have him served.

That was when he knew he had to tell her that he wanted Finell to be his wife instead of her. He remembered Abigail's expression when he told her that he didn't love her anymore. Her face paled, her mouth tightened into a thin line, and her eyes flashed fire.

The night the restraining order was delivered was the last time

David had seen or even spoken to Abigail after telling her that he felt like their getting together was a mistake, that he only meant for them to be in a relationship that was based on mutual sexual desires and not a husband-wife-mommy-daddy kind of situation, and that he was trying to get back with Finell because he was still in love with her.

Abigail, using all her strength, had slapped David and called him several uncomplimentary names. She then turned without saying another word and stormed into their tiny bedroom in their tiny apartment, where she immediately began packing.

Rubbing his jaw, David hunched his shoulders and left the apartment. He needed a few drinks. As he hoped, when he returned, Abigail was gone. The only things she took were clothes for her and the baby. She even left that plain cheap wedding band he had put on her finger when they got married.

It had now been several weeks since she'd left, and to David, it was a sign that he was on the right track with his pursuit of Finell. David thought that Abigail had been nice and a fairly good wife, but she wasn't Finell Everson. In the weeks that followed, he hadn't seen her, but he did receive a letter from her lawyer telling him that she was suing him for divorce, full custody of their daughter, and child support.

It was 11:48 a.m. when David arrived at USI's regional headquarters. He walked in, signed his name at the front desk, and took the elevator to the third floor where Finell worked.

Mrs. Mimms looked at David and coldly said, "Good morning, Mr. Colwins. How can I help you?"

David flashed the scowling woman his most sincere smile; the one that always served him well when dealing with this woman who had always guarded Finell like her own child. "Good morning, Mrs. Mimms. I would like to speak with Miss Everson, please."

NIGHTMARE

"Miss Everson is *Mrs. Hamilton* now, and I'm sorry, but Mrs. Hamilton is not working in this office today. She's working out of the Parker City offices until four o'clock this afternoon. Would you like to leave a message for her?"

Pretending that he didn't know the wedding had taken place, David replied, "So, Miss Everson is Mrs. Hamilton now? I'll be sure to congratulate her when I see her again. No. There's no message. I'll catch her another time."

Turning around, David's smile quickly faded. He wanted to punch the wall. *Finell, you need to stop trying to make things difficult for me, girl!* he thought angrily.

He returned to his car and raced from the parking lot to the southbound freeway entrance.

The Parker City office's production rating had improved to the point where they were no longer on probation. The entire staff was so happy that they presented Finell with a large box of delicious Nuts 'N' Chews candy at the end of the day.

As she was putting the box in her car, she noticed an envelope on her windshield. It was from David: *Dear 'Nell, I've been trying to get with you and we just can't seem to hook up. I haven't been able to catch you at your house. I said that there was something that we needed to discuss, so you really need to meet me tonight at our favorite spot. I know you remember. This is important. I need to see you. We need to talk about our relationship. You can't still be mad. I know that you still love me, and it's time you proved it to me. You need to kick that church boy to the curb so we can get back to where we left off. Call me. Even though you changed your number so that I can't contact you, here's mine. Lovingly, David.*

Finell put the note back into the envelope and threw it on the ground. The icy voice behind her said, "So that's how you feel? You throw my attempts to recapture our love on the ground?"

As David leaned over to pick up the discarded note, Finell tried to get into her car, but David grabbed her by the bun at the base of her head, wrapped his arm around her waist, and began dragging her away from her car.

"No! David, stop!" she screamed. "Don't do this! Please, my husband will be after you for this! Please stop!"

She tried to plant her feet on the ground. He released her hair and wrapped both arms tighter around her body. As he snatched Finell off of the ground, her shoes fell off her feet and she dropped her purse and keys.

"You are mine! You belong to me!" David ranted.

She struggled to get away from him, all the while yelling, "Help! He's trying to kidnap me!"

Finell scratched at his hands and arms, trying to get him to release his hold, kicking her legs and trying to throw him off balance. She fought furiously to get away from David, and that was what slowed him down enough for two men to run toward them.

Remembering that it's difficult to carry dead weight, Finell let her body go limp. She fell backward against his body and threw him off balance.

As the two men running toward them got closer, they began to yell, "Let her go! We're calling the police!"

David had dragged Finell to his truck and was trying to force her inside, but she put her hands on the frame of the vehicle and pushed back. The two men reached them just as David threw her down.

As Finell's head hit the ground, David jumped into the truck, locked the doors, and managed to drive off the parking lot as the men pulled her from the path of the fast-moving vehicle. Finell was on the ground, dazed, bruised, bleeding, and scared.

"Hold on, Mrs. Hamilton, the police and ambulance are on the way," they said to her as she cried, "Call my husband, please!"

While he was in his last meeting of the day, Joshua felt a chill roll down his back and suddenly had an overwhelming urge to call Finell. As he was reaching for his cell phone, it began to chime with Finell's new ringtone. "Hello, babe. Are you okay?"

"Is this Mr. Hamilton?" a man's voice asked.

Joshua's heart skipped a beat. "Yes! Who is this?"

"Mr. Hamilton, this is Officer Gardner of the Parker City Police Department. Someone attempted to kidnap your wife from the parking lot of the USI building in Parker City."

"I'm on my way," Joshua said in a tight voice.

"No. Mr. Hamilton, she's already being transported. You'll have to meet her at Parker City General."

By the time Joshua, EJ, and Finell's parents arrived at the hospital, Finell had already been seen by the emergency room doctor and was waiting to be admitted. When Joshua walked into the room, she tried to smile, but her tears overtook her.

"It was David. He left this on my windshield," she said and showed him the letter. "I've already told the police. This is the original. They have a copy."

Within the next thirty minutes, Finell was admitted to the hospital for overnight observation. She watched her husband as he paced around her room.

"Joshua, go home and get some rest," she told him. "I'll see you in the morning."

Joshua looked at his wife like she was speaking a language he couldn't decipher. Didn't she know that he intended to stay with her?

EJ, who was determined to stay at the hospital as long as he could to be a support for his brother, touched Joshua's shoulder and gently said, "She's right, you know."

Looking at his wife, Joshua said, "Really? You think that I'm going to go home and leave you here?" Then, after showing the letter in his hand to his brother, Joshua said, "Would you go home and leave the woman that you love after reading this?"

Snatching the letter back from EJ, Joshua closed his fist and crumpled the letter into a tight ball.

"Listen, man, let me take care of this," EJ said. "I know somebody who can get this whole situation taken care of tonight."

"Brother, this is my battle, and I'll take care of it myself," Joshua said determinedly.

"So, what are you going to do? Pray about it? This man can't be reasoned with, he needs to be convinced. He needs to know who he's messing with!"

Finell reached out her hand. "EJ, let Joshua handle it, and if what he has in mind doesn't work, then David Colwins is all yours."

After things settled down and the Eversons and EJ had gone home, Joshua gently hugged and kissed Finell. When she fell asleep, he prayed.

"Lord, I need your strength right now. I want to find that man and kill him. But I know that your vengeance on him will be much greater than mine could ever be. Help me to be patient and let Your will be done in this situation. In Your Son's name, I pray and ask all things. Amen."

* * *

Two days later, when Finell was released, there was a car and driver waiting for them. Joshua said, "This is Mitchell, and he is your driver. He will be taking you everywhere you have to and want to go. Mitchell will be with you all day every day from the time you leave home until you return. This is not negotiable."

Joshua sat down on the bed next to his wife.

"Finell, I just want to know that you are safe. Mitch is my friend, and he also wants to help keep you safe from that maniac Colwins. He's very good at things like this, and because we are friends, he's doing this as a favor for us."

Finell looked at the man as he stood near the door of the hospital room. Taking note of his appearance, she saw that Mitchell Craver was a stocky man about three inches shorter than Joshua but obviously heavier, not with body fat but with a bulkier muscle mass.

Joshua further explained that Mitchell was a licensed bodyguard who was registered with the Federal Bureau of Investigation because he was a former agent. Handing Finell a card, Joshua said, "Read this."

The information on the card said that Mitchell was a top-rated marksman and an expert at finding people who didn't want to be found.

Finell looked up at the man and he smiled. "Mrs. Hamilton, I take this job seriously. And if you will allow me, I want to do this for your husband…my friend. And with the amount of money your husband insists that I accept, I intend to be the best chauffeur/bodyguard in the world for you."

After she had been checked out of the hospital, Joshua helped Finell into the back of the vehicle before climbing in behind her. Mitchell Craver closed the door, glanced around, slid into the driver's seat, and they were off.

Finell shook her head. "Josh, I…"

"Fin, baby, I told you that this is non-negotiable."

"But…"

"Mitchell is going to be with you until we find this nut job who won't leave you alone," Joshua said.

As he hid from the police, David Colwins believed beyond a shadow of a doubt that Joshua Hamilton wasn't the type of man to come after him. He figured that if he just laid low for a week, he could return to his quest to get Finell back in his possession. But just to be sure, he waited a while longer before trying again.

CHAPTER 13

Finell and Joshua were celebrating another month of marriage. Finell's heart swelled when her husband had a bouquet of red roses delivered to her office with a love note attached that made her cry.

Earlier that morning, she "flipped the script" and woke Joshua up by touching, kissing, and whispering intimately to him, initiating a robust round of early-morning lovemaking, after which she made him his favorite breakfast.

Tonight was USI's thirty-fifth-anniversary banquet. This would be their first major social outing since the wedding. Whatever stubborn vestiges of scrapes and bruises she'd sustained in the accident would all be covered by her long-sleeved, midnight-blue, floor-length gown with gold trim around the high neckline, wrists, waist, and hem.

Joshua, of course, thought she was beyond beautiful in the fitted bias dress that flared from just above her hips to the floor. Finell doubted that any man would look more handsome than her husband in his midnight-blue tuxedo with a gold vest and gold accents.

David Colwins had successfully evaded the police for the past several weeks. He was determined to get Finell back in his life. His original plan had been to follow her around thinking that he could just wear her down. But he was forced to back off so the police wouldn't get him before he could talk to her again. All he wanted to do was to show her that he wasn't easily discouraged. He intended to explain everything to her once she was back with him.

He hadn't meant to hurt her, but when he realized she was not going to meet him like he asked her to, he lost his temper. He merely acted out of fear tinged with a little anger, he told himself.

Although David thought he'd outsmarted the police, he didn't know that Mitchell Craver had him in his sights. There were several times that Mitchell could have "taken him out," but Joshua had given orders not to touch him. His orders were to find David, follow him, report his whereabouts, and keep him away from Finell.

The bad part about the whole situation, David lamented to himself, *is that I couldn't get into her hospital room to apologize because of all those police officers roaming around. Then the church boy got her that chauffeur.*

Tonight, David would make one final attempt to talk to Finell. He just wanted some time to plead his case and make her see things his way. She was his, and he was going to make her understand it once and for all. In his mind, he was left with no other alternative but to show up at the banquet.

He stood in the shadows as much as he could and watched her flirting with Joshua.

She's trying to make me mad. I don't want to have to hurt her! he thought as he watched them.

"Mr. Hamilton," Mitchell Craver reported, "the target is in the building."

Joshua looked alarmed. "Call the police. Keep watching him, and I'll watch my wife. When he makes his move, we'll get him."

"Yes, sir, Mr. Hamilton," Mitchell Craver said.

NIGHTMARE

Finell and Joshua were having a good time. They danced, laughed, and enjoyed themselves. When they returned to their table to rest, Finell excused herself. As she exited the restroom, David was leaning against the wall and waiting for her.

"Hey, 'Nell. You look presentable. Let's get out of here."

Finell released a mirthless laugh as she backed away from David. "Get away from me. You know I'm not going anywhere with you."

David looked at her like he couldn't believe what she was saying. He stepped close and raised his finger to her face. When she smacked his hand away, he snarled through gritted teeth, "Who do you think you're talking to?"

Joshua, EJ, and Mitchell Craver were standing back, watching the exchange. When David's hand went up, Joshua moved, but Mitchell grabbed him and whispered, "Be patient, boss, we won't let him hurt her."

Finell stepped away from David and started walking back toward the ballroom. "I know who I'm talking to, you don't scare me. How did you even get in here? Why don't you leave me alone?"

David grabbed her arm and spun her around. "I said let's go! I'm sick of you trying to flaunt that Bible-thumping rebound in my face. You're coming with me and you are going to do everything I tell you to do, got that? You belong to me, so like I said, let's go! Now, *GET GOING!*"

Behind him, David heard a low, cold, hard voice. "You need to get your hands off of her. And I'm not going to repeat myself."

With his jaw tightly clamped and his heart racing, Joshua slowly moved toward them. With each step, he prayed, *Father, please protect her. Don't let him hurt my wife.* He fought hard within himself not to raise his voice or make any sudden moves.

David released Finell and turned to face Joshua. "You think I'm afraid of you? Well, you need to think again." Without warning, he lunged forward.

Joshua was ready as the man propelled himself at him. It was a huge surprise to David when Joshua's fist struck his abdomen with enough force to double him in half and lift his feet off the floor.

Wanting David to know that he had made a serious mistake by continuing to harass Finell— by disrespecting him on the telephone, by putting her life in danger, by trying to kidnap her, and by coming here tonight to manhandle his wife—Joshua jammed his elbow into David's back between his shoulder blades.

When David was down in a ball on the floor, Joshua stood over him. "This is the last time I'm going to tell you to stay away from my wife." He reached down and grabbed the fallen man by the collar and dragged him to his feet. "Do you understand me?"

"You can both go to hell, you deserve each other," David gasped. "A loner and a frigid fat bi—"

Before he could finish, Joshua's fist smashed into David's face. He went spiraling back into the wall and crumpled to the floor. But Joshua was not finished. He bent down and lifted David to his feet again. With one hand clamped around his throat and the other gripping David's collar, Joshua repeatedly slammed the man against the wall until his arms were too tired to continue doling out more of the punishment.

Mitchell Craver put a hand on Joshua's shoulder. "Mr. H, I think you've finished teaching the man a lesson."

EJ rushed toward Joshua to keep him from permanently injuring the fallen man, but Mitchell waved him off.

"This is one time that your little brother can handle his own business," Mitchell said. Then, slapping cuffs around David's wrists, he said, "Hey, Colwins. I bet you had no idea when you woke up this morning that the preacher man was going to beat you like a drum and crumble your aspirations to dust, did you?"

Joshua stepped to Finell, took off his jacket, and wrapped it around her. She was trembling when Joshua folded her to his chest and whispered in her ear, "It's okay, don't worry. I'm right here, and he's not going to bother you ever again."

When the police arrived, Finell handed them a copy of the restraining order against David. As the eyewitness reports were being taken, EJ whispered to his brother, "You go ahead and get her out of here. We got this."

Finell pulled her husband's jacket tight around her body and leaned on his shoulder as he led her to the door of the banquet hall. Everyone was watching and whispering.

Myra stopped her son at the door. "Why are you even involved with someone like her? She is so beneath you, son."

"Shut up, Mother, and get out of my way."

Myra gasped. "What has gotten into you? You've never talked that way to me before!"

Edwin Sr. took his wife by the arm and said, "Leave the man alone, Myra." Then he nodded at Joshua. "Go ahead and take her home, son, we'll take care of everything here. You just take care of your wife."

Joshua helped Finell into the car and they drove home. It was a long, quiet ride. When they got home, Finell opened the passenger-side door and stepped out. Joshua caught up with her at the front door.

When he took hold of her shoulder and turned her to face him, Joshua saw the sadness in her eyes when she said, "Your mother's right, Josh, you're out of my league. You deserve to be with someone who doesn't come with so much baggage." She sighed as she searched her handbag for the door keys so that she wouldn't have to meet his gaze.

Joshua took the keys and put them in his pocket. "Stop talking foolishly. Let's go inside."

Finell didn't move. "Your mother is right," she insisted. "You don't deserve to be around someone like me."

He cradled her face in his hands. "I've waited a long time for God to bless me with a wife. There were times when I didn't think my prayers were being heard. Then you came into my life. I knew the first time I saw you that you would be my wife."

Joshua picked her up and carried her into the house and up the stairs.

"You were a victim," he said, "but you don't have to worry about that man anymore. No one blames you for his actions. David Colwins is going to get what he deserves for his actions against you. He has so many charges against him that I believe he could be looking at a long prison sentence."

They walked hand in hand up to the second floor. When they reached the bedroom door, he gave her a kiss on the forehead and hugged her tightly, hoping she would be assured that the worst of things were over.

"Now let's not even think about him anymore. He's already occupied too much of our time together. From now on, let's just focus on each other."

CHAPTER 14

Finell couldn't believe her marriage was a year old. So much had happened in that time. The most harrowing were the incidents with David. She was thankful that the whole situation had finally come to an end.

David was given a harsh sentence as a result of several things, including the bench warrant that had been issued against him, as well as his violation of the terms of the restraining order and the attempted kidnappings.

Finell and Joshua expressed their concern for David's mental stability and asked the court through their attorney if David could receive counseling during his incarceration.

The couple celebrated their special day at a honeymooner's resort. They had a wonderful time. Now here Finell was six weeks later, standing in her bathroom and looking at another at-home pregnancy test wand. The plus sign was showing. She could hardly believe that she and Joshua were going to be parents.

"Oh, my goodness," she whispered through her tears. "I've got to find a special way to tell Josh. He's going to be so happy."

She was supposed to be getting ready to leave for her winter catalog photo shoot. Now she found herself wondering how she was going to tell her agent, Sheila, that she would be taking a leave from modeling until after she had the baby.

I know she'll be happy for me, but I don't want her to be put at a disadvantage because of me, Finell thought.

Sheila was the director of the S.R. Mack Agency and a friend of Finell. The women had met when Finell was in college and Sheila was her academic adviser. It was Sheila who'd convinced Finell that she should take a job as a plus-size model to help finance her college career.

When Finell took her advice and was awarded a job as a full-size model, Sheila became her manager. Then, as her career advanced even more, Sheila became her agent. They'd been friends ever since.

I'll just have to come right out and tell her that I'm retiring from modeling, Finell thought, licking her lips nervously. *She'll understand. I hope.*

Finell took a shower and dressed for work. Joshua had already left the house. He had a meeting with the board scheduled in the afternoon and had gone in early to ensure everything was in place and set up correctly.

She was glad he was gone. She'd made an appointment with her OB-GYN and didn't want him to know about it.

It was seven thirty-five in the evening when Joshua finally came home. He was worn out, and all he wanted to do was go to bed, but first, he had something he wanted to discuss with Finell.

As soon as he stepped into the house through the garage door, he sniffed something that tantalized his olfactory lobes. When Finell walked up to him and offered him a kiss, he smiled. "Hey, babe, you got it smelling good all up in here."

She was so happy to see Joshua. "Hey yourself. I'm glad to see you. I've missed you all day."

In a weary voice, Joshua said, "Babe, I'm going up to take a shower, and when I get back, we need to have a quick conversation."

While she was waiting, Finell set the table with her special china, gold flatware, and crystal candle holders with gold candles. She was excited to tell her husband, the future Daddy, their good news.

"Wow, everything looks nice, Fin," Joshua said, standing in the archway of the kitchen. He walked over to her, took her hand, and led her to the bench of the breakfast nook.

"I see you're already packed and ready to leave tomorrow for your photo shoot," he said. "But I want to know how much longer you intend to continue with this modeling stuff?"

"Well, I do enjoy it, but…"

"But what? I want to know when you plan to stop. It bothers me that you're gone for a week and sometimes longer playing dress-up around who knows what kind of people and having your picture taken in things that sometimes look a little suggestive and improper for the wife of a minister."

Finell tried to pull her hands away from his, but he gripped them and held them close so that she couldn't stand.

"No, wait a minute, hear me out, please," Joshua said. "I've been thinking about this for a while, and I want to get this said before you leave me tomorrow. You're a married woman with responsibilities that have to be put on hold every time you go away. I think this needs to be your last time. You should tell the Mack Agency to get themselves another girl." Thinking the conversation was over, Joshua released her hands and stood. "Something really smells good, and I'm starved. Let's eat."

"No, no," Finell said, "I don't think we're ready to eat just yet. I have a few things to say. First, I like modeling, and I'll decide when and if I'm going to stop working in that field. Second, you know that I take care of all of my responsibilities before I leave.

And—"

"And nothing," Joshua interrupted. "This discussion is over. I've made my decision. No more modeling. That's non-negotiable."

"What? Wait a minute, where is this coming from? What do you mean by non-negotiable? Who do you think you're talking to, Joshua?" Finell's voice was trembling. "You don't make those kinds of decisions for me."

Joshua was trying to hold onto his temper. It had been a long day, and he had been looking forward to spending a quiet evening relaxing. But he had to let her know that he was tired of her leaving him. "Listen, I don't feel like any drama tonight. You need to be obedient about this. Because if you're not, then you may as well not bother to come back to my…"

Finell stepped up to him. "Are you going to tell me that if I don't bow down to your commands that I shouldn't bother to come back here? Is that what you're about to say to me?"

Joshua didn't answer. He couldn't believe that he'd almost said something so ridiculous to his wife.

Finell looked him up and down and pursed her lips. "Mmm-hmm, and I really thought you were different. Well, I'll tell you what. How 'bout I leave tonight before I say something that I'm going to regret?"

"Finell, wait," Joshua said, but she didn't stop, and he didn't go after her. He just stood in the middle of the kitchen. He heard her go upstairs and come back down. He heard her leave the house by the front door. He heard her open the garage door, pull her car out of the driveway, and drive away.

After spending the night at the Airport Traveler's Inn, Finell boarded the plane the next morning with a heavy heart. EJ, her brother-in-law and pilot, said "You know that your husband has been calling me all night, don't you?" Finell only shrugged. "He's worried about you, girl, and he's sorry."

She laid her head back and closed her eyes, trying not to cry. She didn't think she had any more tears left, but she was wrong. "Thanks, EJ. When do you think we're going to take off?"

Knowing that she was politely telling him to mind his own business, EJ headed for the cockpit. As he was preparing for takeoff, he sent a text to his brother: *She's here. She's fine.*

* * *

Sheila met Finell at the gate when her plane arrived. "Ooh, girl, look at you. What happened?"

"Not now," Finell said. "I don't feel like talking about it. Excuse me." She cut the conversation short and ran to the restroom. Her morning sickness was starting early today.

Two days later, after a long day of shooting, Finell was tired of wearing the restrictive evening wear that she'd been modeling. She didn't feel very festive, and all she wanted to do was get back to her room and rest.

After a short nap, she awoke to the sound of someone knocking on the hotel room door. It was Shelia.

"Hey, Sheila, how are you doing?" Finell said and tried to smile.

"I'm doing just fine," Sheila answered, and added, "I just finished talking to your too-fine brother-in-law, and he says that you and your husband had a fight."

"That's my business, and I won't discuss that. But I do want to tell you that I'm pregnant."

Sheila grabbed her arm, but Finell wouldn't let her talk.

"Please," Finell begged, "please don't tell anyone. My husband doesn't know yet."

Sheila was shocked. "Why not? He should have been the first one to know! Stop playing around and tell the man. Ooh, you young girls are somethin' else."

"He doesn't know because we had an argument before I could tell him."

"Listen, girl. Argument or not, you better tell that man as soon as you get home. Just 'cause he's crazy don't mean you have to act that way too. You know he acts that way because he can't help himself. Men are just naturally senseless anyway. But I heard he's a good man, so whatever the argument was about, just forgive him." With that, Sheila pulled Finell into a tight hug. "Get your rest, and I'll see you later for the evening shoot."

The rest of the shoot went extremely well, and by the following Friday morning as the models and the crewmembers were boarding the plane to return home, everyone was tired—but Finell was just plain worn out. She was exhausted, tired of being sick, but most of all she was tired of being mad at her husband.

Before preparing for takeoff, EJ sat down beside Finell to talk to her.

"Listen to me, sister-in-law, I need to tell you that your husband is in bad shape. The whole time you've been down here, you haven't answered one of his text messages or even answered any of his calls. I bet you haven't even listened to any of his voice messages. The man is about to lose his mind, so I told him that we're scheduled to arrive home by three o'clock. And just so you can get yourself together, I'm letting you know that he's going to be there waiting for us." Standing quickly, EJ patted her shoulder and headed for the front of the plane.

* * *

NIGHTMARE

Joshua watched Finell as she walked slowly across the tarmac, pulling her suitcase with her carry-on bag over her shoulder. Instantly Joshua was relieved and very glad to see her.

Looking closely at his wife, he noticed that she was thinner. Her eyes were puffy and red. Her complexion was pale, almost sallow. To him, his wife looked exhausted, like she was ready to drop. Joshua immediately felt guilt-ridden because he knew that he was partly responsible for her current state of being.

As she stepped into the terminal, Finell's attention immediately turned to her husband. She noticed everything about him. He looked thinner. His eyes were sad. And his smile was uncertain.

Finell felt a little sorrowful as she looked at him. How could she have treated him so badly? She thought to herself, *The very least I could have done was to send him a text message or even answer one of his voice messages. How could I have been so cruel to the man that I love so dearly?*

Joshua met her as she stepped around the partition. As she drew near, he reached out and relieved Finell of her luggage, but they didn't touch, and neither offered the other a hug or a kiss.

"You didn't have to come," she informed him. "I engaged a service."

"I canceled it," he responded.

"I'm not going to your house," Finell said.

Looking intently at her, Joshua stepped in her path and stopped walking. When their eyes met, he spoke softly but sternly. "You won't be staying in a hotel tonight." Then, stepping to the side, he added, "We are going home together!" as he touched her lower back.

She tensed but didn't move away or offer any more disputations. His hand felt so good to her as he rested it on her back. She almost let herself relax at his touch. She wanted so badly to turn and hold him in her arms, but she didn't know if he would accept her gesture of love.

At home, she grabbed the handle of her suitcase and rolled it through the house, pulling it up the steps and rolling it down the hall to the guest room farthest from the master bedroom suite.

Joshua smiled secretly and followed her. In the guest room, he dropped her carry-on bag onto the hope chest bench at the foot of the bed. "How long do you plan to stay in here?"

Without turning to look at him, she stated, "Until I find an apartment."

He turned and walked away. As he was leaving the room, he said, "Well, you're going to be in here a long time, because that apartment thing is not ever going to happen."

Joshua spun around when the shoe she threw whizzed past him and hit the floor in front of him. He quickly walked back into the room and put his hand against the door so that she couldn't slam it in his face.

When Finell stepped back, he stepped through the doorway and gently captured her arms in his hands. "You know, I missed you too. I'm so sorry." He pulled her to him and kissed her with all the pent-up passion he had been holding in while she was gone. "I'm thankful that you're back here with me. I can't sleep when you're not here. I'm so tired. I want to hold you. Just for a little while."

She put her arms around him and he cradled her in his arms as he carried her across the room and lowered both of their bodies to the bed. He kissed her again and held her to his chest. It wasn't long before they were asleep in each other's arms.

* * *

The weekend started out slow and cautious. They woke at midnight, hungry, and ate in the kitchen. Afterward, they returned to

NIGHTMARE

the guest bedroom where they reaffirmed their love for one another, showered, and went back to bed.

Joshua and Finell were both bone tired and overjoyed to be back together. As they were lying in bed, Joshua sang "If Only For One Night" to Finell while she fell asleep. The next time they awakened, it was ten thirty Saturday morning.

Finell opened her eyes slowly and lay as still as she could for a few moments, then sat up gingerly. That was no deterrent to the morning sickness that quickly overtook her. She tried not to make too much noise, but Joshua was already awake.

Afterward, she brushed her teeth, rinsed her mouth, washed her face, combed her hair, checked herself in the mirror, and thought that she looked like nothing was wrong. But as she opened the bathroom door, what she saw made her stop short. Joshua was waiting for her. Without saying anything, he picked her up and carried her down the hall to their bed in the master suite.

Pulling back the quilt, Joshua helped her settle under the covers, resting her back on the pillows he had fluffed against the headboard. He smoothed the covers over her lower body and handed her a ginger ale and a few unsalted crackers.

"Now, don't you have something you want to tell me?" Joshua asked.

Finell sipped the room-temperature drink and ate a few crackers, letting them settle her roiling stomach. She saw the big grin on his face and asked, "How did you find out?"

Joshua looked at her softly. "Tell me, Finell. I want to hear you say the words to me."

She looked at his face shining bright with excitement and lifted her hands to cup his face. "Joshua Hamilton, I am pregnant. We are going to have a baby."

He leaned forward and whispered in her ear, "Thank you.

Thank you. I love you so much. Those words speak volumes about our union. I love you so much." He climbed onto the bed and settled her in front of him between his outstretched legs.

Smiling, she asked again, "How do you know? How did you find out?"

He pulled her back against his chest and wrapped his arms around her shoulders. "How do I know? I know because I recognize and appreciate everything about you."

He ran his hands from her shoulders to her arms and wrapped his arms around her waist. She settled back against his chest.

"Your body has made some subtle changes," Joshua said. "When I hold you, you feel softer. When I kiss you, you taste sweeter. When you talk, your voice has music in it. When we make love, it's more intense, more pleasurable, and more satisfying." He kissed her shoulder. "Besides, while you were gone, it dawned on me that you'd missed your last two cycles. And with this morning's sickness, I was hoping."

She took his hand, raised it to her mouth, and kissed it.

Joshua said, "My love for you has grown so much that my heart can hardly contain it. At this moment, I am so thankful to God for you and the amazing blessing He has gifted us with. Our baby, Finell, is an answer to our prayers."

She felt his chest heaving and heard him catch his breath. Moving out of his lap and crawling to the middle of the bed, she pulled him to her and held him to her chest as his tears wet her sleeping gown.

"I was going to tell you the night that we argued," Finell said. "My bags were packed, but I was going to call Sheila and let her know that I was going to retire. I was going to show you these."

She took an envelope from her side table drawer and handed it to him. Inside was a series of sonogram images of their baby and

NIGHTMARE

three EPT wands indicating she was pregnant.

Together, they whispered to each other, "We're having a baby."

Kissing passionately, they were intensely affectionate toward each other for several more hours.

* * *

Because it was Saturday, Joshua insisted that Finell stay in bed while he worked in his den on the message that he was going to deliver the next day for his ordination service. Finell was more than glad to slide under the covers and nap. Her bouts of morning sickness left her feeling like she'd just worked a twelve-hour day.

Finell didn't wake up until two o'clock, and it was half an hour later when she came into the kitchen. She stopped short when she saw her parents, Joshua's parents, and EJ sitting at the table. Everyone greeted her at once.

"There she is!"

"How you feeling, baby?"

"Well, hello, young lady!"

"Welcome home."

"What are you all doing here?" Finell said as Joshua stepped up beside her.

"We wanted to see if you two had made up yet," EJ said. "I didn't think either one of you was going to make it through another night apart. You were both in bad shape."

"Oh, we made up," Joshua said happily. Then he turned to Finell. "Babe, say those two words for me again, please."

Everyone was staring at her. She beamed at Joshua and lightly slapped his arm. Then, with her hand on his cheek, she looked into his eyes and said, "I'm pregnant."

The three men jumped up and began shaking Joshua's hand and

pounding him on the back. The two women stood and moved across the room to hug Finell.

Myra took her by the shoulders. "My dear, sweet daughter-in-law. I have never seen my son as happy as he has been since he met and married you. Thank you for being just what he needs as a companion. I love you, Finell, and I hope you can forgive me for all the problems I've caused and the thoughtless words that I've said. Please forgive me."

Finell tearfully replied, "Of course I forgive you, Mrs. Hamilton."

Karina Everson folded her daughter in her arms. "My baby is having a baby. I'm so happy for you."

CHAPTER 15

After an intense examination by the ordination committee, Joshua stood behind the podium in the main sanctuary of the Good Samaritan Church in his black robe and spoke one word into the microphone: "Forgiveness."

He looked around and let his eyes rest on his mother.

"To give pardon, to exonerate, and if you will, to show mercy. Forgiveness is an act of love unconditional."

Myra looked at her son and dropped her eyes to her hands as he continued.

"I have to forgive myself so that I can forgive others, so that I can accept God's forgiveness. I need to forgive others so that God will forgive me. Today, I stand before you as a forgiven man. And especially as a man who has forgiven others."

Joshua next let his eyes settle on Finell.

"Forgiveness is an act of love. Forgiving yourself and others shows that you have accepted God's love into your heart and you are more than willing to share His love with all. As humans, we are imperfect. And because of our imperfections, we are all sinners. Yet when we pray, repent, and ask for God's forgiveness, He does not tarry in the process.

"So, if He can forgive us, we therefore should forgive others. Because as we navigate through this life, we must realize that we are sinners who have fallen short of the glory of God, and without his forgiveness, we would not have hope. No one is perfect, and a lack of forgiveness is detrimental to your spiritual well-being. Forgive so that you can be forgiven."

Then he quoted several scriptures.

"Matthew 6:14-15. 'For if you forgive men when they sin against you, your heavenly Father will also forgive you. But if you do not forgive men their sins, your Father will not forgive your sins.'

"Colossians 3:13. 'Bear with each other and forgive one another if any of you has a grievance against someone. Forgive as the Lord forgave you.'

"Ephesians 4:31-32. 'Get rid of all bitterness, rage and anger, brawling and slander, along with every form of malice. Be kind and compassionate to one another, forgiving each other, just as in Christ God forgave you.' "

Before he closed his sermonic message, Joshua stepped out of the pulpit and offered Finell his hand. When she stepped into the aisle, he put his arm around her waist and let it rest lightly on her abdomen.

"During our courtship, and for the first few months of our marriage, my wife was being stalked. Eventually, the man was arrested and has been sentenced, but despite that, the man needs forgiveness. So last night during our prayer time, Sister Hamilton and I forgave him, and we also prayed that he would come to know God in the pardon of his sin and ask for God's forgiveness himself."

Joshua shifted Finell behind him, helping her to sit back in the pew. He continued down the aisle, stepped in front of his mother, and said, "So brothers and sisters, if you have someone in your life who needs forgiveness, or if you need forgiveness from someone, now is your time. Don't let this moment pass without seeking or offering forgiveness."

He leaned forward and kissed his mother's cheek.

"I forgive you, Mom. Will you forgive me?" he whispered.

Stepping to the middle of the center aisle, he raised his arms. "Now is the time, brothers and sisters. Get up. Step out into the aisles. Find that someone you need to forgive or ask for their forgiveness. My sisters and my brothers, let's forgive. Ask for forgiveness. And receive the true blessing of God's forgiveness."

With that said the congregants all but ran from the pews, seeking and being sought by other members of the church. There was crying, hugging, shouting, dancing, laughter, prayers, and spiritual healing.

Pastor Brown was pleased to see that his son in the ministry was able to get the members of the congregation to a point where they were asking to be forgiven, offering forgiveness, and praising God through dancing, singing, and shouting words of thankfulness to God. Smiling broadly, the pastor recognized that Joshua's first Sunday morning sermon was uplifting, informative, and inspiring, as well as having just what was needed to set the church on fire.

As Joshua returned to the pulpit and brought the message to an end, the members of the ordination committee laid hands on him; they gave him his charge and offered prayers for him and his family. After that, Pastor Brown stepped to the rostrum and was the first to congratulate Joshua as he was awarded his certificate of ordination.

The church hosted a reception for the newly ordained Reverend Joshua Hamilton. It lasted two hours. By that time, Finell was almost too tired to stay awake.

"Come on, babe," Joshua said, "let me get the two of you home. And when we get there, I'm going to rub your back, sing to our baby, and hold you until we fall asleep."

Finell looked up at her handsome husband and asked, "Can I have some kisses, too?"

"Oh, Mrs. Hamilton, there will be kissing and lots of other things to go along with them."

Joshua and Finell laughed as they walked out of the church reception hall holding hands.

ABOUT THE AUTHOR

G. Louise Beard was born in Baltimore, Maryland. The second of five children, she earned a B.S. in Special Education from Coppin State College. She and her family relocated to Ogden, Utah, where she earned an M.Ed. in Secondary Education from Weber State University.

An avid reader, she spent her early years dreaming of becoming a writer, however the necessities of life—marriage, raising a family, teaching, becoming a minister/pastor's wife—took priority and kept the dream at bay.

Now in retirement, she is taking advantage of the opportunity to fulfill her dream of becoming a published author. She is the author of the books *Right Next Door* and *Mail Ordered*.

www.ingramcontent.com/pod-product-compliance
Lightning Source LLC
LaVergne TN
LVHW091047100526
838202LV00077B/3060